# KINGDOM

# OF

# FIRE AND FAE

*By*

*J.E. Taylor*

Cover Art by Adrijana Cernic

# KINGDOM OF FIRE AND FAE

Welcome to Solstice City—a realm where floating markets dazzle beneath the luminescent glow of rune-powered streetlights. And destiny's threads entangle Lanae and Draven in a perilous weave.

In a world teetering on the brink of chaos, Lanae and her brother confront their gravest challenge yet. Alestain Firetwill has resurfaced, commanding an army ensnared by his sinister mind control, turning allies into adversaries and family into fierce foes. Racing against time, the siblings must break their parents free from Firetwill's grip before they're forced into a heart-wrenching battle against their own flesh and blood.

Meanwhile, Draven embarks on a treacherous journey to reclaim the fabled Dragon's Heart. With Solstice City freshly risen from its ashes, the city's fate now hangs by a thread. Should Draven falter, the city will be reduced to cinders once more.

As fire clashes with fae, and magic intertwines with love, the power of family, courage, and loyalty is put to the ultimate test. Can these bonds withstand the overwhelming darkness? The fate of Solstice City—and the world—rests in their hands.

Dive into this electrifying conclusion where every whisper hides a secret, and every shadow might conceal an ally—or a foe. Perfect for fans who crave intricate characters, lush world-building, and plots that keep you on the edge until the very end.

# CHAPTER ONE
## *Solstice City Reborn*

AS DAWN BROKE OVER the rejuvenated Solstice City, its cobblestone streets glistened with the first light of day, thrumming with newfound energy. Lanae Nightshade wandered through the bustling markets with her brother Caelum, their footsteps resonating against the stone paths. The aroma of freshly baked bread and exotic spices filled the air, mingling with the distant sound of merchants hawking their wares. Vibrant banners and colorful awnings fluttered in the gentle morning breeze while the sunlight danced off the polished marble of the surrounding buildings. The crowd was a kaleidoscope of cultures, with vendors showcasing their handmade crafts and produce.

Lanae's eyes sparkled as they stopped at a blacksmith's table, eyeing some of the newly crafted swords on display. The sun gleamed off the polished blades, casting a dazzling array of reflections. She admired the intricate engravings on the hilts and the craftsmanship of each piece.

"Don't you think you have enough swords?" Caelum asked as he fiddled with the pommel of his new Solstice City guard sword, the fresh leather strap of his sheath creaking with each movement. His newly minted uniform, crisp and immaculate, made him stand out among the crowd.

Lanae side-eyed him, and pride filled her. Today was his first day out of training. She just hoped it would be much less eventful than her first day during the height of the war with the dark fae.

"You can never have enough swords." Her lips turned up in a grin.

Since they had defeated Xoltan Firetwill, there had been no more attacks from the dark fae. They had sent a missive to the council that they would like to start the peace process. The parchment had arrived sealed with an unfamiliar sigil, and she had been given the honor of delivering it straight to the council.

Draven had scoffed when she told him, but he still carried a monstrous chip on his shoulder against all fae. Well, all besides her and Caelum. At least he came to a truce with Faide and the council after Caelum had recounted what Draven had done to the gauntlet stone and his participation in defeating the dark lord.

A shadow crossed over the table, and she looked up into those intense green eyes that held her heart. Draven Emberwing was a force of nature all on his own. His commanding presence sent a shiver of excitement through Lanae. His crimson hair, tousled by the morning breeze, framed his chiseled features.

"Another sword?" He echoed her brother's words, his deep voice reverberating through the air.

Caelum snickered beside her, the sound almost swallowed by the bustling market around them. He reached out to inspect one of the knives, its blade gleaming under the morning sun, and he paused, drawing a sharp breath.

Dread filled Lanae, and she shot her gaze to her brother's face. That vacant look she remembered from the mind-control machine graced his expression, but the assault of his emotions in her mind confirmed her brother was still inside his head. Unlike what had happened in Xoltan's court, where his expression had been truly empty.

His gaze cleared, but the unfiltered terror in his eyes as he looked at her squeezed her chest like a vise. His knuckles turned white around the knife handle before he released it with a clatter.

He blinked and swallowed hard, glancing between her and Draven. "I think our reprieve is over." Even his words shook, a tremor that echoed the fear pulsing through the telepathic connection he had with Lanae.

Caelum hadn't had a vision in years. With him coming of age, his unique powers were coming into their own, and as a little kid, he had been prone to random spells, as their parents called them. But seeing his vacant look brought those memories back with a vengeance.

"What did you see?" She faced him, her heart thumping in a wild timpani beat.

"Mom and Dad reanimating." He glanced toward their house, where they had imprisoned their catatonic parents after the war with Xoltan. All Xoltan's mind-controlled minions had fallen into a catatonic state, waiting for another Firetwill to take control of them again. The house, once a sanctuary, now loomed like a prison.

Draven pulled him away from the vendor stall. "You have visions?"

"I used to get them a lot when I was little, but they stopped when I hit puberty." Caelum ran his fingers through his hair, the motion quick and agitated, a clear divergence from his usual calm demeanor.

Lanae put her hand on his forearm and squeezed, but her stomach knotted. "Do you know how long we have?"

Caelum shook his head, his eyes unfocused. "Weeks. Days. Hours. I don't know." He turned toward the Citadel, the one building that wasn't structurally destroyed by the attempt at merging realms. It still stood stoically in the center of the city as a symbol of their resilience. "I need to warn the council."

"I'll check that the safeguards are still in place at home," Draven said, his jaw set. "Go with your brother."

Lanae leaned up and pressed her lips to Draven's. That familiar tingling of their fate bond rolled through her body, a momentary comfort to the turmoil roiling her abdomen. "Thank you."

She headed away from the shiny swords with Caelum by her side. Her mind raced with worry.

Perhaps Caelum's first day might be even more daunting than hers was, after all.

# CHAPTER TWO
## *Guard Duty*

CAELUM FIDGETED BY LANAE'S side as the Fae Council flowed into the ornate room, their robes trailing behind them like the tails of comets. Golden light filtered through the stained-glass windows, casting colorful patterns on the polished wood floor. This was the first time Caelum had been before the entire council, and nerves bit at the edges of his palms, making them itch.

Faide Frostvale, the head of the Fae Council, settled into his seat, his presence commanding attention even among the esteemed assembly. His violet eyes, sharp and knowing, locked onto Caelum with an intensity that made him shift uncomfortably.

"You have news?" Faide's voice was calm, but the underlying authority in his tone was unmistakable.

"Not news exactly." Caelum glanced to Lanae for support, his sister's presence a comfort amidst the storm of his anxiety. Lanae's expression was serene, betraying none of the turmoil radiating through their bond.

"My brother had a vision." Lanae's voice rang out clear and strong, the acoustics of the grand hall magnifying her words so they bounced from wall to wall, echoing in the ears of every council member.

Faide's eyebrow rose, and he leaned forward, the movement almost predatory in its focus. "Well, spill it, boy."

Caelum chewed his lip, trying to formulate a more politically correct way of delivering the message, but the urgency of the situation made him abandon decorum. In the end, he just blurted it out. "Alestain Firetwill is awakening his forces."

Six words.

And every council member paled, their stares turning to the empty seats. The once-vibrant council now had positions still vacant, haunting reminders of those who had succumbed to Xoltan Firetwill's mind-control machine. The silence that followed was thick with dread, each member's face a reflection of the collective fear that gripped them.

Faide's fingers drummed on the table, breaking the heavy silence. "We have prepared for this moment for the past three years." His words dripped off his tongue in a measured calm that belied the magnitude of the situation. "Please notify the senior guards and have them meet us in the situation chamber.”

Caelum swallowed hard, the reality of his vision’s implications settling like a lead weight in his stomach. He glanced at Lanae, who gave him a reassuring nod. They had a battle ahead, and every second counted.

“Yes, sir.” He turned with Lanae at his side and headed out of the council chamber. Caelum’s mind raced as he and Lanae descended the winding staircase, the echoes of their footsteps a rhythmic token of the urgency of their mission. The grand corridors of the council building bustled with activity, unlike the last time Caelum had graced these halls. Council assistants hurried past, their robes a blur of colors, while guards stood at attention by every doorway, their presence a constant indicator of the ever-present need for vigilance.

A shudder throttled his spine at the memory that surfaced, the stark contrast between now and then making him uneasy. Lanae gave him a questioning side-eye, her brows knitting together in concern.

“Just remembering the last time I was in this part of the building.” Caelum’s voice was just a whisper as the memories threatened to overwhelm him.

“After the battle with Xoltan?” Lanae’s tone was soft, but there was an edge to her words, a shared understanding of the pain they had both endured.

He shook his head, a rueful smile tugging at the corners of his lips. “No. When you were tried for treason." His words were heavy with the weight of the past.

Lanae's eyes softened, and she reached out, briefly squeezing his hand in silent support.

He surveyed the number of people moving through the corridors, noting the determined expressions and the sense of purpose that permeated the air. "It's a lot busier now."

"Well, they moved all the city offices here. It isn't just the council anymore," Lanae explained, her gaze sweeping across the bustling scene. "The administration, logistics, and even the intelligence units are all centralized here now. It's become the heart of Solstice City's governance."

Caelum nodded, taking in the transformation. The once solemn and almost deserted halls were now alive with activity. As they continued their journey through the corridors, the memories of the past faded, replaced by a dread that made each footstep heavy.

As they crossed the threshold into the bustling streets of Solstice City, the vibrant energy of the metropolis enveloped them. Children laughed and played in the squares, and street performers entertained clusters of onlookers with their skills.

Caelum's thoughts, however, were far from the lively scene around them. His brow furrowed as worry gnawed at him. "What if we aren't completely free of their influence?"

Lanae let out a breath, her gaze warming as she looked at him. "We are," she reassured, though her tone carried a hint of exhaustion.

"But what if we aren't?" He stopped abruptly, grabbing her arm and making her meet his intense gaze.

"Caelum, we both were freed by Nero's magic. It severed the hold that bastard had on us." Her firm voice rang through the air and she placed a hand on his shoulder, a placating gesture that set him on edge.

"I haven't had a vision for years. So why now?" His voice wavered, carrying hints of fear and confusion. He glanced around, taking in the thriving city that had once been on the brink of despair.

Lanae sighed, and her eyes reflected her empathy as much as their telepathic bond. "Maybe it's because the need is greater now than ever. Visions come when they're most needed, Caelum. Perhaps Nero's magic awoke something within you that lay dormant until now."

Caelum's grip on her arm loosened, and he nodded slowly; the worry clutching his belly eased. He looked at the city around them, the people who depended on them, and a renewed sense of resolve to keep all he held dear safe flared. They had overcome so much already, and with Lanae by his side, he knew they could face whatever challenges lay ahead.

LANAE SCANNED THE CITY as they made their way to the guard barracks to inform the generals that they were needed at the Citadel. Her mind turned over Caelum's question. Even though she had told him Nero had broken Firetwill's hold over them, his query had burrowed under her skin. The bustling streets below, filled with the clamor of preparation, seemed a world apart from her inner turmoil.

At the barracks, they relayed their orders to the gathered generals. The air was thick with urgency as the leaders nodded in understanding, their expressions grave. The looming threat was tangible, and there was no room for hesitation.

Once the messages were delivered, she and Caelum exchanged a brief but significant nod. "Stay sharp," he murmured before they parted ways, each heading to their respective stations.

Lanae made her way to the training grounds. The rhythmic rattle of weapons and the shouts of warriors greeted her as she arrived. She scanned the area, her eyes landing on a familiar figure, who she had closely trained with over the last couple of years.

Jenna, one of the formidable women warriors, was in the middle of an intense training session. Her movements were almost as precise and powerful as Lanae's, which made for a good sparring partner. The clash of their swords echoed through the training grounds, drawing the attention of nearby warriors who paused to watch the impressive display. As the bout ended, Jenna removed her helmet, revealing a crop of blonde hair with purple highlights and a smile of accomplishment.

Lanae approached, ready for an outlet to work out the anxiety still stiffening her muscles. "Are you ready for a real sparring session?"

Jenna rolled her eyes playfully. "Give me a second to get a drink and then I'll kick your ass."

Lanae let out a bark of a laugh, the sound carrying across the training grounds. "When have you ever kicked my ass?"

"You never know. Today may be that day." Jenna grinned and sidled up to the cooler for a drink of fresh spring water. She took a long sip, seeming to savor the refreshing flavor before wiping her mouth with the back of her hand. "Besides, I've been working on some new moves. You might be in for a surprise."

Lanae raised an eyebrow, intrigued. "New moves, huh? Well, I'm always up for a challenge."

Jenna's smile widened as she set her drink aside and picked up her sword. "Good. Let's see if you can keep up."

Lanae squared off, waiting for Jenna to make the first move. When it came, she parried, striking the sword away with little effort. The rest of the guard gathered closer, eager to witness the friendly yet fierce competition between two of the Citadel's finest warriors.

DRAVEN SLID INTO THE house and stopped in the entry, tilting his head to listen. At first, only silence reached his ear, then a scratching sound came from the back of the house. His brow furrowed in suspicion.

"Nero, you better not scratch up that door again!" he called out, his voice echoing through the quiet house. With a resigned sigh, he closed the front door and strode through the hallway toward the kitchen.

Upon entering the kitchen, Draven found Nero perched on his bed, the picture of innocence. The griffin's large, soulful eyes blinked up at him, as if to say, "Who, me?" But the wood shavings scattered across the floor told a different story.

Draven crossed his arms and tapped his foot, raising an eyebrow at the griffin. "Seriously, Nero? We've talked about this."

Nero cocked his head to the side, letting out a small, pitiful squawk. Draven couldn't help but smirk at the theatrics.

"You're not fooling anyone with that look." Draven bent to gather the shavings. "You know, if you wanted attention, you could just ask. Instead, you turn our doors into toothpicks."

As Draven swept up the mess, Nero shuffled closer, nudging his head against Draven's arm. The affectionate gesture made Draven chuckle despite himself.

"All right, all right. You're forgiven." He gave Nero a scratch behind the ears. "But seriously, buddy, if you keep this up, we're going to run out of doors."

Nero let out a rumbling purr, clearly pleased with himself.

Draven shook his head, unable to stay mad at his mischievous companion for long. As he finished cleaning up, he glanced toward the main suite in the house where they had locked up Lanae's parents.

"Any noise from the bedroom?" Draven nodded toward the door, his expression turning serious.

Nero shook his head, a low growl rumbling in his throat as if to confirm that all was quiet.

"Good," Draven said, and the knot in his stomach released. "The last thing we need is more trouble."

Nero's wings fluttered and his tail thumped against the floor, agreeing with Draven's sentiment.

Draven gave Nero one last affectionate pat before heading toward the bedroom to check on Lanae's parents. As he moved, he muttered under his breath, "You know, for a griffin, you sure know how to make a mess."

Nero chirped in response, his eyes twinkling with mischief.

Draven couldn't help but laugh. "Yeah, yeah, I love you, too, you big troublemaker."

His skin itched with anxiety as he stopped in front of the door. He wiped his sweaty palms on his trousers and shook his hands to loosen his muscles before reaching up to the top of the doorframe to retrieve the key. It was hidden among the cobwebs and dust, a seldom-used relic. With a deep breath, and a twist of the key, he unlocked the door, hearing the faint click that seemed louder than it should be in the silent hallway. He opened the door; the hinges creaked in protest, and he peered in.

The room was dimly lit by a single candle. Lanae's parents still lay prone on the bed, their breaths shallow and rhythmic, untouched by the passage of time. The air brimmed with the fragrance of aged linens and a faint trace of lavender, a remnant of happier times. He stood there for a moment, watching them with a pang of helplessness.

He shut the door gently and locked it again, returning the key to its dusty perch. He walked back to the kitchen, his footsteps echoing in the narrow hallway. "I need to go let Lanae know that her parents have not woken. Did you want to come?"

Nero, who had been lounging in the corner, nearly pounced on him. The griffin was no longer the tiny creature Lanae had found years ago. Now, he was the size of a pony, his powerful body rippling with muscle. His head reached just shy of Draven's, and his wingspan was almost as wide as the kitchen itself. Soon, they would have to figure out an alternative nest outside rather than the oversized bed that took up the entire corner of the kitchen. Nero's golden eyes gleamed with excitement, his beak clicking softly in anticipation.

The people of Solstice City had become used to seeing Draven walking with Nero. The two enigmas in a city of varying species were a familiar sight, yet they never ceased to draw curious glances: Draven, the last dragon, with his unsettling presence and piercing green eyes, and Nero, the majestic griffin, an ancestor of the first griffin, and a symbol of strength and mystery.

Draven gave Nero a stern look, his brow furrowing as he took in his walking companion. "Don't even think about showing off today. It's already been a trying morning, and I don't think Lanae would be pleased if you set your storm loose." His voice carried a weight of authority, but also a touch of weariness.

Nero squawked in response, his feathers puffing up as he rolled his eyes. The griffin's expressive face illustrated his defiance, but also a hint of playful mischief. He shifted his weight from one taloned foot to the other, a clear sign he was brimming with restless energy.

Draven side-eyed him and exhaled, the sound filled with resignation. He knew Nero too well; the

griffin would likely test all their patience before
the day was done.

17

# CHAPTER THREE
## *Rebellion and Revelation*

THE MOMENT JENNA FAILED to block her sword, Lanae's eyes sparkled with determination as she pulled back just before the blade touched the skin of Jenna's neck. Her grin widened at her sparring partner. "It looks like I won again." Her voice carried a teasing lilt.

"Damn it," Jenna muttered under her breath, dropping her sword with a clatter that echoed through the training grounds. She trudged over to the cooler, her steps heavy with frustration, and grabbed another drink. The sound of the ice shifting in the cooler contrasted their earlier tension.

"You're getting better." Lanae stepped beside her, her fingers brushing against the cool metal of the cooler before she grabbed a drink for herself. The cold liquid was a welcome relief, soothing her dry mouth and tired muscles. This time, it took her longer to defeat Jenna. "That spin away move was impressive," she added, the compliment genuine.

Jenna met her gaze, a flicker of pride in her eyes. "Thanks." She finished her drink in one long gulp and crumpled the paper cup, tossing it into a barrel under the cooler. "So, how are things with your dragon?" She waggled her brows with a playful grin.

"Good as always." Lanae's smile was brief, a mere shadow of her usual warmth. Caelum's vision had soured her mood, and the sparring session hadn't dispelled the dark cloud hanging over her. If anything, it had compounded the pressure. They all had to be ready for the next attack, and she wasn't sure all the guards would make it out of this next war alive. She started to step away, but Jenna's hand on her arm stopped her.

"What's wrong?"

Lanae glanced down at Jenna's hand, the warmth of the touch contrasting with the cool air, and then met her gaze. "The peace we've had might not be for much longer." As if to punctuate her words, a shadow passed over the sun, casting a fleeting darkness over the training grounds.

"What happened?" Jenna asked, concern etched on her face.

But Lanae was no longer listening. Her lips pressed together in a thin line as she spotted Nero doing rolls in the air above the training grounds. As he came out of the last one, a web of lightning cracked through the air, the sharp sound startling the nearby guards.

The soldiers on the training field ducked and covered their heads, their armor clinking softly.

"Lanae!" one of the elite guards overseeing the training in the absence of the generals yelled with annoyed authority.

"Nero!" Lanae called, her voice cutting through the noise. The griffin swooped down, soaring close enough to her head for the rush of air from his wings to ruffle her hair. She caught the mischievous glint in Nero's eyes as he passed over her, the griffin's laughter almost audible in his gaze.

Draven jogged across the field, his boots thudding against the ground, and stopped by her side. "Sorry. He needed to get out of the house before he ruined the door again," he said, slightly out of breath but with a rueful smile.

Lanae palmed her face, the tips of her fingers pressing into her temples as she peered through her fingers at him. "Really?" Her voice was a mix of exasperation and disbelief, her eyes narrowing.

Draven smirked, the corner of his lips curling up in that familiar, nonchalant way. "Your parents are fine, by the way. No indication of motion at all." His tone was casual, almost as if discussing the weather.

Relief sagged her shoulders, the tension draining away. "Thank you for checking." Her tone took on a soft hush.

She sent the information to Caelum through their mind link, the sensation like a gentle brush of feathers in her consciousness. Just as she finished, Nero dive-bombed the group again. The echo of his wings sliced through the air like a whispering storm. This time, he clasped a soldier by the arm with his talons, lifting him a few feet off the ground before releasing him. The soldier yelped in surprise, his armor clinking as he landed.

"You had to let him out?" She waved a hand toward the rebellious creature, her frustration bubbling to the surface.

"I told you long ago that griffins are notoriously unstable," Draven replied, his smirk never fading.

"He's not unstable. He's just acting out." She stabbed her gaze in Nero's direction.

The griffin hovered in the air, his eyes gleaming with mischief. His feathers rustling in the wind were almost a challenge, daring her to say otherwise. The sun glinted off his pastel plumage, creating an almost ethereal glow around him as he circled back for another pass.

This time, when Nero swooped down, Lanae extended her arm and shot vines from the soil. The thick, green tendrils coiled around his talon with a serpentine grace, pulling him to the ground. Nero squawked loudly, the sound echoing off the nearby trees, and he narrowed his eyes at her, a mix of surprise and irritation flashing in his golden gaze.

She approached him, her boots crunching on the dry leaves and twigs scattered across the training ground. Wagging her finger, she fixed him with a stern look. "This is not a time for fun and games. We need to train without you terrorizing us. Wait for Firetwill's forces to get here, and then you can let your full powers strike."

Nero's beak snapped shut with an audible click, and the feathers on his head ruffled, standing on end. A low rumble emanated from his chest, resonating through the air. The sound was almost like a distant thunderstorm, echoing his raw power. The mention of Firetwill's name had triggered his protective instincts. The griffin's memory of the man who nearly destroyed his newfound family burned fiercely in his mind.

Nero's eyes reflected his fierce protectiveness, mixed with a desire to release his pent-up energy. She sighed softly, reaching out to pat his feathered neck, running her fingers over the warm, soft down. "Soon, Nero," she whispered, her voice gentle. "But for now, we need to stay focused."

"I NEED TO GO. I'm supposed to be meeting Varkir at the bar." Draven stepped beside Nero and glanced at Lanae. "Did you want me to take him back home?" He hooked his thumb at the griffin.

"He really needs to exercise." Lanae glanced at the troublemaker, her furrowed brows threaded with touches of irritation and concern. "Are you going to behave and go hunting?" Her voice was firm, but there was a softness underlying it, a plea for cooperation.

Nero nodded his head and chirped, the sound a high-pitched melody that filled the air.

"No livestock." Draven pointed at him, his finger stern and unyielding. "Understand?" The memory of the previous debacle flashed in his mind, the chaos and cost of smoothing over the outrage regarding the mystical teenage predator.

Both he and Lanae had laid into the beast, their voices raised in frustration as they yelled at him about his piss-poor actions. The echo of their words still seemed to linger until the creature had taken to the skies. Nero had come back a while later with talons full of gold, the glint of the coins catching the sunlight. If Draven had to guess, he would have bet Nero had gone back to the Isle of Dreams, where he got the medallion that had awakened his powers, and cleared the place of coin.

The griffin's wings fluttered, the feathers rustling like a whisper in the wind, but he inclined his head, agreeing to Draven's terms. The vines Lanae had bound him with released, slithering back into the soil. Nero took flight, the powerful beats of his wings creating a gust of wind that rustled the surrounding leaves. He banked over the outer walls, heading to the woods where deer and wild boar were plentiful.

Draven leaned down, his eyes softening as he stole a kiss from Lanae. That tingle that flared any time they touched cascaded through him like a balmy shower, heating him from the inside. Her lips were warm and familiar, and although he wished to linger there, she was on the training field and unless he picked up a sword to spar, he was intruding on her practice. "I'll see you at home later. If anything changes..." His eyes scanned the walls, their gaze sharp and attentive, and then returned to hers, filled with an unspoken promise. "Send Nero to get me."

The sound of Nero's wings beating faded into the distance, leaving a sense of relief from the guards hanging in the air.

He turned and strode off the field, the burning of the eyes of every guard drilling into his back like hot coals. Over the last few years, he had sparred with Lanae on occasion and impressed even the seasoned veterans on the guard. The clang of swords and the grunts of exertion still echoed in his ears. But even if they wanted him on the force, he wouldn't agree because mistrust of the fae still lingered in his heart like a shadow that refused to fade.

When he entered the newly built tavern, the scent of fresh wood and spilled ale greeted him. He crossed to the bar, where Nicoli, the sexy djinn bartender, was mixing cocktails for a rowdy group. The clinking of glasses and the hum of conversation filled the air. As he slid into his seat, the leather creaked under his weight. She looked up at him and grinned, giving him a head nod of acknowledgment. Her eyes sparkled with mischief, but she had learned over the past couple of years not to push him for wishes. Despite her and Lanae being longtime friends, it still took Lanae's serious threat to slit her throat to stop her from flirting with him.

The tavern was alive with energy, the laughter and chatter of patrons creating a lively atmosphere even at this early hour. The flickering candlelight painted shifting patterns on the walls, enveloping the room in a cozy glow. Draven drew a lungful of air. The scent of roasted meat and spices mingling with the faint hint of Nicoli's exotic perfume and alcohol permeated the place.

It didn't take long for a trail of smoke to sail through the door, curling and twisting through the air before materializing in the seat next to him. The smoke coalesced into a humanoid form, and Varkir's smile settled on his face as he went from ethereal to corporeal in a matter of seconds. His arrival was accompanied by a faint scent of sulfur and a whisper of warmth.

At least this time, his clothing wasn't a tattered mess like the first time they met. He wore a neatly pressed dark tunic and trousers, the fabric clean and free of any rips or stains. Since freeing him from Firetwill's clutches, the yôkai had cleaned up enough that even his natural gray pallor didn't look so sickly. His hair, once matted and unkempt, now fell in smooth, sleek strands around his angular face.

"What news do you have for me?" Draven asked, his voice low but filled with curiosity and a hint of urgency.

Nicoli slid a drink in front of each of them, the glasses clinking softly on the wooden bar top before she dashed off to address another patron. The amber liquid inside caught the light, casting a warm glow between them.

Varkir took a moment to savor his drink. He swirled the liquid thoughtfully before taking a sip, his eyes meeting Draven's with a twinkle. "I've managed to gather some information about the Dragon's Heart."

His voice still had that ultra-smooth quality that made Draven second-guess whether or not to trust him. It was the kind of voice that could either soothe or deceive, and the uncertainty gnawed at him. But the man knew how to dig up information, and he had been loyal to Solstice City and Lanae ever since his return from imprisonment. The sound of clinking glasses and murmured conversations filled the space around them, a backdrop of noise that ratcheted Draven's tension. The low hum of the tavern, mixed with the occasional burst of laughter, created an almost claustrophobic atmosphere.

"And?" he asked when Varkir didn't continue. His ire rose enough to produce smoke from his nostrils. The faint tendrils curled into the air, dissipating quickly.

"And you are not going to like it." Varkir fidgeted in the seat, toying with his drink before chancing a glance at Draven. His normally confident demeanor was replaced with unease, his fingers tapping nervously against the glass.

Draven took a breath, cooling down the aggravation that simmered just below the surface. "I won't kill the messenger." He smiled, though it was tight-lipped and strained. "Out with it."

"Well, it seems the Dragon's Heart no longer carries any magic or power. It's just another defunct talisman that Alestain wears like a badge of honor." Varkir's words came out in a rush, as if getting them out quickly would lessen the blow. He took a gulp of his drink, nearly draining the cup.

Icy dread filled Draven's chest, the sensation like a heavy boulder settling in his stomach. He had been counting on that damn stone to help him fully shift like he could as a child. Losing that hope was a crushing weight. "How is that possible?" he asked, the words laced with disbelief and desperation. The room closed in around him, the noise fading to a dull roar in his ears as the reality of Varkir's news sank in.

"I also found information relating to ancient documents about the Dragon's Heart that might give you some glimpse into what drove the power in that relic," Varkir said, his voice tinged with cautious optimism.

Draven stiffened and turned fully toward Varkir, his eyes narrowing as he processed the words. "You could have started with that," he retorted, his voice edged with irritation.

Varkir chuckled, the sound a low rumble that seemed to vibrate through the air. He shrugged, a nonchalant gesture that belied the seriousness of the situation. "I'd rather leave you with hope than deal with your moody devastation," he replied, his eyes twinkling with mischief.

Draven didn't know whether to throttle the man or pat him on the back. The stress in his body eased, and a mix of frustration and gratitude swirled within him. The noise of the tavern seemed to recede, leaving a bubble of focused conversation between them.

Varkir's expression softened, his gaze earnest and unwavering. "My sources mentioned these documents are in a language that no one can decipher, so their ideas of what it might or might not contain are just hearsay," he explained, his tone serious now, each word measured and deliberate.

Draven's mind raced, the possibilities and risks flickering through his thoughts like a whirlwind. The revelation settled heavily on his shoulders. "Where is it?"

The flickering candlelight cast dancing shadows on Varkir's face, highlighting the uncertainty etched into his features, the play of light and dark emphasizing the somber reality of their conversation.

"It's not in this realm. But I've asked my people to bring it to me," Varkir replied, his voice steady but laced with the tension of the unknown.

"Thank you." Draven raised his glass to his friend, the liquid inside catching the light and shimmering like molten gold. He downed the drink in one smooth motion, the fiery liquid burning a path down his throat and lighting a fire in his stomach. The sensation was a strong juxtaposition to the cold dread that had filled his chest moments before. The warmth spread through him, igniting a resolve that had been smoldering within.

Hope—no matter how tenuous—was a beacon he couldn't afford to ignore.

# CHAPTER FOUR
## *Magical Breech*

LANAE AND JENNA HEADED toward the mess hall to grab a bite before they went to their respective stations throughout the city. The midday sun cast long shadows, and the air was infused with the aroma of grilled meats and fresh bread wafting from the army kitchen. Their footsteps echoed in the cobblestone streets, accompanied by the distant clamor of the bustling city.

A lone elite guard approached them, his armor gleaming in the sunlight with every powerful stride. His gaze locked onto Lanae, a penetrating look that made her skin prickle. His physique came close to that of Draven's: wide shoulders, a broad chest, arms built to break, and powerful legs that seemed capable of snapping necks if he so chose. His crop of golden hair glistened like a halo, but his eyes were as dark and foreboding as Xoltan Firetwill's.

"Mmm." Jenna licked her lips audibly as she scanned the elite guard. The sound broke the silence like a whip crack, making Lanae's heart jump.

"Lanae Nightshade?" His deep voice rumbled as he stopped before them.

"Aww, you always get the sexy ones," Jenna muttered, her voice laced with amusement.

Lanae threw her a look, annoyance flickering in her eyes, and then nodded at the guard. She thought she knew all the guards, elite or otherwise, in Solstice City, but she had never laid eyes on this one before. There was something unsettlingly familiar about him, yet alien at the same time.

"Granger Spiritwalker." He moved his hand in a crisp salute, the motion sharp and practiced. "You are needed in the situation room."

Lanae returned the salute, her eyes narrowing with suspicion. "I don't believe I've met you before."

"I've been traveling the realms for some time on council business," he replied, his gaze shifting to take in the city around them, "and came back to Solstice City recently." He glanced around at the city with a strange mixture of nostalgia and wariness. "It has changed a great deal since the last time I graced these streets."

"When was the last time you were here?" Jenna asked, still standing by Lanae's side, her tone curious but cautious.

His brow furrowed, and a shadow crossed his face. "It's been eleven or twelve years."

"So, before the peace talks fell through." Lanae's intuition prickled as he nodded. There was a heavy silence, broken only by the distant cries of hawkers in the market and the rustle of leaves in the breeze. "What type of business does the council have in other realms?"

He smiled, but it didn't reach his eyes. "Collecting allies."

"And the realm you were in was not impacted by the near merge three years ago?" Lanae pressed. She had seen the damage that caused to the fae realm and that of the seer, and couldn't imagine what other realms looked like after they stopped the destruction.

He let out a laugh, the sound harsh and grating. "That's when I attempted to get back to Solstice City, but that proved difficult and communications between realms were nearly destroyed."

"Oh." His answer appeased some of the anxiety making her skin itch, but it didn't completely dispel the unease. "Well, shall we?" She waved for him to lead the way. "See you in a bit," she said to Jenna.

Jenna gave her a wink and walked away. "Have fun!" she called over her shoulder, her voice echoing through the narrow streets.

*I doubt the council situation room will be anything close to fun.* Lanae's thought bounced into her mind, and then she focused on the presence next to her. His footsteps fell in rhythm with hers.

He glanced at her, his expression unreadable. "I heard you were the one who ended the siege."

"I was there." She didn't want the credit for overcoming that evil. Draven had insisted to the council that Lanae be awarded the accolades and not him. He wanted to remain in the shadows because of the danger of the Dragon's Heart.

"Your humbleness is unexpected." He raised an eyebrow, his gaze piercing. "Taking down a tyrant is something to brag fiercely about." A smile toyed on his lips, but there was an edge to it.

"Yes, well, all the death and destruction that Firetwill caused..." She stopped speaking and shook her head, the memories weighing heavily on her mind. "It's not something I enjoy reliving," she finally said.

"I guess you never get over taking a life, even if it is in the midst of war."

"Exactly."

Once they were out of view from the guards, Granger led her onto a side street that headed toward the Citadel. The narrow alley was shrouded in shadows, and the distant murmur of the city seemed to fade away. Before they stepped onto the main thoroughfare, Granger grabbed Lanae's arm, his grip firm and unyielding, and tossed a vial on the street before them. A sharp, hissing sound filled the air, and a portal opened, sucking them through the ether.

DRAVEN RETURNED TO THE house to find Nero in the backyard with a small deer carcass. The coppery tang of blood mingled with the earthy aroma of the forest surrounding them. Nero glanced up when Draven cracked the back door to check on him, the sound of the creaking hinges cutting through the quiet afternoon.

"Nice catch," Draven said, his voice strained but attempting to sound casual. He was glad Nero wouldn't be eating them out of their meat supply for a day or two. The glimpse of the fresh kill was a grim indicator of the harsh reality they lived in.

He inspected their food supply, the cool air from the storage pantry hitting his face as he opened the door. Pulling out ingredients for dinner, his mind raced with all that Varkir had told him. A weight settled on his chest, heavy and suffocating at the thought of never being able to shift into his full dragon form again. The kitchen seemed too small. The walls closed in on him as the enormity of the situation sank in.

Caelum strolled in as Draven set the roast he was making in the oven. "Lanae's not here?" He looked around, his voice a sudden intrusion in the tense atmosphere. "Huh." He closed his eyes, and a crease of concentration appeared, deepening with each passing second. The silence was thick, punctuated only by the crackling fire in the hearth.

When Caelum's eyes opened, Draven's heart fell with a bang into his stomach. "What?" Dread coiled around his insides.

"It's like she's not here. I can't reach her." Caelum's voice was tight with worry, his normally calm demeanor cracking.

If Lanae was shutting her brother out, that meant she was in trouble. Draven shut off the oven with a sharp click and grabbed his sword, the cold weight of the weapon grounding him. He cracked the back door and stared at Nero, who was still working on his meal. "Lanae's missing."

Nero dropped the meat immediately and took to the skies, his powerful wings beating against the air with urgency. Draven closed the back door, the finality of the sound echoing in the empty kitchen, and stalked to the front of the house where Caelum waited at the open front door, tension radiating from him in waves.

"Last I saw her, she was on the sparring field with Jenna." Draven crossed the threshold, with Caelum by his side. He closed the door behind them, locking the house up tight as if to keep the looming dread at bay.

"I think Jenna might be at Mystic Spirits with a few of the guards," Caelum said, his voice tight, the concern mirrored in Draven's own heart. The tension between them was deep, a silent agreement that finding Lanae was their top priority.

They headed toward the bar, each step filled with mounting anxiety. The streets were alive with the sounds of the city winding down for the evening, but Draven's mind was consumed with thoughts of Lanae. Caelum's inability to reach his sister tied knots in Draven's stomach. Every instinct in Draven screamed at him to find Lanae, to protect her from whatever shadows lurked in the corners of their world.

Mystic Spirits was hopping with guards and fae looking for a refreshment at the end of a busy workday. The raucous laughter and clinking of glasses filled the air, creating a marked disparity to the unease gnawing at Draven's insides.

Draven scanned the bar, his eyes darting from table to table until his gaze landed on Jenna sitting with a half dozen other guards. The candlelight played across their features, shadows darting and shifting, yet there was no mistaking Jenna. She was laughing at something one of the guards had said, her smile bright and carefree.

"Jenna!" Draven called out, his voice cutting through the din of the bar. The conversation at their table halted, and Jenna's head snapped up, her wide eyes locking onto Draven's.

Draven and Caelum made their way over to the table, the urgency in their stride unmistakable. "Jenna, we need to talk," Draven said, his tone leaving no room for an argument.

Jenna's smile faded as she took in their serious expressions. "What's going on?" she asked, concern creeping into her voice.

"Lanae's missing," Caelum said bluntly, his eyes scanning the room as if hoping to catch a glimpse of his sister.

Jenna's eyes widened, and she stood up abruptly, the chair scraping loudly against the floor. "She was with me on the sparring field earlier, but then she got called away by an elite guard." Her voice was tinged with worry.

Draven's jaw tightened. "We need to find her now."

Jenna's brows furrowed. "The guard's name was Granger Spiritwalker. He said she was needed in the situation room. He seemed familiar, but I couldn't place him."

Caelum's eyes narrowed. "Spiritwalker... I don't like the sound of this. We need to check the situation room."

Jenna nodded, determination replacing the worry in her eyes. "Let me know if she isn't there." She reached out and squeezed Caelum's hand.

Caelum nodded. "I will."

As they left Mystic Spirits, Draven's heart spurred into a gallop, and he prayed they would find Lanae safe and unharmed.

THE MOMENT THEIR FEET hit the ground, Lanae's heart rampaged in a feral beat in her chest as she struggled to reach her sword. Granger's grip was like iron, and he easily stripped the steel from her grasp. With a forceful shove, he sent her stumbling backward. Her foot caught on a bump in the floor, and she crashed to the ground, the cold, hard surface jarring her bones. Bars slammed shut with a deafening clang, caging her in a cell.

"What the hell?" she spat, scrambling to her feet. She launched herself at the cell door, her fingers clawing through the opening between the bars. An icy fear scraped across her skin, sending a jagged tremor down her spine.

Granger's hand shot out, grabbing her wrist and yanking her arm against the bars. His feral smile sent a chill of fear through her. Pain seared through her skin where her skin touched the cage, and the acrid stench of burning flesh filled her nostrils. Her skin sizzled, and she yanked back, cradling her arm to her abdomen. Her eyes widened in horror as she took in her surroundings. The room was hauntingly familiar, the unanimated forms frozen in time around her like macabre statues. Every breath was laden with the stink of decay, and a cold sweat broke out on her forehead.

"A fitting iron prison for a murderess," he sneered, his voice dripping with contempt.

Lanae's chest throbbed violently, each beat echoing in her ears like a war drum.

Granger walked around the cage as he inspected his palm with a casual indifference that sent a rake of shivers crawling down her spine.

"I must be going, but when I return, your punishment will begin," he continued, his voice a chilling promise. "Before the war is through, you'll be begging me for death."

His cold, piercing eyes flicked up to meet hers, and for a moment, it appeared he could see straight into her soul. The air around her grew colder, and she wrapped her arms around herself, trying to ward off the chill.

As Granger walked away, his footsteps echoed in the silent room, each step punctuating her impending doom. She was left alone with the fae statues, their lifeless eyes staring at her, their expressions frozen in time. The oppressive air swirled, steeped in the scent of decay and fear. Lanae's breath came in shallow gasps, her mind racing as she tried to escape this nightmare.

CAELUM LED THE WAY to the Citadel, the air thick with tension. As they ventured closer to the situation chamber, the cold, stone walls seemed to close in on them, amplifying their footsteps. The guards in front of the door straightened, their eyes narrowing in suspicion as they pinned Caelum and his companions with a look that usually would have had him turning around and avoiding the confrontation. But this was his sister's well-being, and he needed to know whether she was in that room or not.

The sharp bite of metal armor and the musty odor of the ancient building filled his nostrils, and Draven's anxiety rolled off him in waves, sparking his own unease into a frenzy. The cold air bit at his skin, and his breath came in short, sharp bursts. Nero stalked next to them, his movements predatory, as if hunting for his next meal. The silence was deafening.

"Have you seen my sister?" Caelum asked with desperation.

The guards glanced at each other, their expressions unreadable. "Our shift just started a half hour ago, and no one has come in or out of the room," one of them replied, his voice flat and emotionless.

"We were told Granger Spiritwalker escorted her here earlier today," Caelum insisted, his throat tightening with fear.

Their eyes blinked in unison. "Granger never showed up for his shift," the guard on the right mumbled.

Caelum's throat tightened further, a lump forming as panic threatened to overwhelm him. "Can we please see if she is in there?" he pleaded, his voice trembling.

The guards hesitated, their eyes darting back and forth.

The air grew colder as the situation pressed down on Caelum's shoulders. The shadows in the hallway seemed to stretch and lengthen, creating an oppressive atmosphere that made it difficult to breathe. His heart worked itself up, each beat echoing in his ears as he waited for their response. The world around him seemed to fade away, leaving the unbearable tension and the desperate need to find his sister.

Draven's growl rumbled through the air, a guttural sound that made the hairs on the guards' arms stand on end. The metallic rasp of swords being drawn echoed in the corridor, but it was Nero who snapped first. With a flash of electrifying blue, he surged forward, his lightning crackling and causing the guards to dive aside, their faces contorting in fear. The scent of ozone and burned hair drifted in the air as Nero reared up, his talons gleaming menacingly. When he slammed his front talons into the door, the wood splintered and the hinges screamed in protest before the door flew open, crashing into the wall with a thunderous boom.

Inside the room, conversations ceased mid-sentence, and every head swiveled toward the source of the commotion. Faide's eyes narrowed as he straightened, his fingers twitching toward his own sword. He glared at the massive griffin and Draven standing defiantly in the doorway. The room's occupants were a sea of wide eyes and slack jaws, and Caelum's heart thrummed wildly as he scanned the crowd, frantically looking for Lanae. His breath hitched when he couldn't spot her.

"Where is my wife!" Draven's snarl was more than a question—it was a promise of chaos. His eyes darted around the room, every muscle in his body coiled tight like a spring ready to unleash fury.

Caelum's heart when haywire. He knew Draven's secret nuptials had been a bombshell waiting to drop. Lanae had kept it from the council and the guard, not wanting to rock the boat. The council's disapproval was the least of their worries now.

"What did you say?" Faide's voice was a low, dangerous growl as he stepped closer, his eyes flashing with barely contained anger.

The tension in the room was thick enough to cut with a knife. A door at the back of the room creaked open, and all eyes snapped to it. Lanae stepped out, and her eyebrows rose at the collective attention. Before Draven could utter a word, Faide's fury was directed at her.

"You married him without the council's blessing?" Faide's voice was sharp, his finger jabbing at Draven as if his very presence was an affront.

Lanae's eyes widened, her mouth falling open in surprise. She blinked rapidly, like a deer caught in the headlights, before she gathered herself and squared her shoulders. She might have been startled, but Lanae was not one to be easily cowed.

Caelum reached out to Lanae telepathically, desperate to connect, but found only silence. His heart flailed. She had blocked him, just as she did on the battlefield. His mind flashed to another setting where she kept him out: the bedroom. He could still remember the mortifying moment he had heard her moan in his mind—he had practically begged her to block him then. The battlefield he could handle. But her intimate moments? No, thank you.

The room buzzed with nervous energy, the silence heavy with unspoken threats and simmering anger. This was far from over.

"Perhaps you should head home with your husband, Lanae." Faide's tone left no room for debate, his voice as cold and unyielding as a glacier.

Lanae opened her mouth, the faintest breath of protest escaping her lips, but Faide's icy glare silenced her immediately.

"Go home. Now. We will discuss your situation as soon as we have a solid plan of attack." His words struck with the finality of a judge's gavel.

Lanae's shoulders sagged for a moment, but she quickly composed herself and strode to the door, her footsteps echoing in the tense silence. As she passed by the trio, her eyes flicked to Caelum, fury reflected in her irises, and Caelum felt sorry for Draven and the fireworks that were sure to go off the moment they entered the house. Nero squawked loudly, his keen eyes daring anyone to challenge them further, his feathers puffing up in agitation.

"Come on," Caelum muttered, grabbing Draven by the arm and steering him away from the hostile stares that bore into their backs like daggers. "Before you get me in trouble, too."

Draven's jaw was clenched so tightly that his teeth might have cracked under the pressure, but he allowed himself to be led away. An unmistakable tension charged the air, thick enough to choke on, and the magnitude of every unspoken word pressed down on them.

Nero gave one last indignant squawk, as if to say, "This isn't over," before following Lanae, his claws clicking ominously against the floor.

Lanae remained silent, the tension simmering just below the surface, a powder keg waiting for a spark.

A BONE-WRINGING CHILL ran through Lanae as the room grew darker, the shadows creeping across the polished marble floor like grasping fingers. She sat in the middle of the cage, her knees drawn to her chest, utterly exposed and on display. The chill in the air seeped into her bones, making her tremble uncontrollably. Her gaze flicked to the empty bucket in the corner, a stark reminder of her humiliating predicament.

As the day wore on, the growing pressure in her lower abdomen became impossible to ignore. She glanced around the room, her eyes lingering on the motionless figures. None of them moved a muscle, all still trapped in the mind-control coma, just like her parents. The eerie stillness was both a curse and a relief; at least no one was watching her every move.

With a resigned sigh, Lanae gave in to the inevitable. She slid her pants down to her ankles and squatted over the bucket, closing her eyes as her urine emptied from her bladder. The sound of the liquid hitting the metal echoed in the silent room. She bit her lip, fighting back tears of frustration and humiliation.

As she buttoned her pants back up, her stomach let out a loud, rumbling protest. The hunger gnawed at her insides, a relentless ache that refused to be ignored. She wondered how long she would be subjected to this silent torture, deprived of food and water, with only a bucket to relieve herself in. Each passing minute crawled like an eternity, the gnawing fear and uncertainty growing stronger with every second.

Desperation clawed at her as she tried to summon her magic. She focused her thoughts, willing the vines to burst through the marble floor to give her some semblance of control in this nightmare. But just like the last time she was in this hellish place, nothing stirred. Her magic lay dormant, unresponsive to her pleas.

The cold, unyielding marble beneath her seemed to mock her efforts, its smooth surface a vivid contrast to the wild, untamed power she sought to unleash. The room remained deathly silent, save for the faint rustling of her clothes and the distant drip of water. The oppressive darkness pressed in on her, magnifying her sense of dread.

Hours passed, and the gnawing sensation of hunger took hold. Her stomach growled incessantly, the sound echoing in the silence like a beast demanding to be fed. She pressed her hand to her belly, trying to quell the growing discomfort. Her throat was parched, each swallow painful as if she were trying to gulp down shards of glass. The metallic tang of the stale air hung heavy in the cell.

Deep-seated dread crept over her, curling around her thoughts like a dark, suffocating fog. Her mind raced with questions and fears, each one more terrifying than the last. *What was happening outside these walls? What plans were being made?* The uncertainty was maddening, and a knot of anxiety tightened in her chest.

She tried to reach out to Caelum telepathically, but there was nothing but an empty void. The lack of connection was disorienting, rendering her more isolated and vulnerable. She closed her eyes, trying to center herself, but the darkness only seemed to magnify her fears. Every creak and rustle in the cell clanged like a harbinger of doom, making her heart launch into high gear.

Draven's image floated into her mind. His determined eyes and fierce love made her hope flare. But even that hope was tinged with fear. *What would he do to get her out? What would he sacrifice?* The questions swirled around her mind, each one adding to the growing sense of dread.

She hugged her knees to her chest, trying to find some warmth and comfort in the small gesture. Her breaths came in shallow, ragged gasps, and she fought to keep her emotions in check. The cell closed in on her. The walls pressed tighter and tighter until she couldn't breathe.

Lanae had faced countless battles and dangers, but this—this waiting and uncertainty—was a different kind of torture. The physical discomfort was nothing compared to the mental and emotional agony of not knowing what lay ahead. And as the hours ticked by, her situation pounded down, threatening to crush her spirit.

The hours dragged on, each one more torturous than the last. Hunger, thirst, and fear gnawed at her, wearing down her resolve. The silence was maddening, every sound amplified in the suffocating darkness. Lanae closed her eyes and tried to block it all out, clinging to the hope that somehow, some way, she would find a way to break free.

# CHAPTER FIVE
## *The Encroaching Darkness*

DRAVEN FOLLOWED LANAE'S POUNDING footsteps, each step echoing through the dark corridors like a drumbeat of impending doom. He kept a safe distance, not daring to approach her while the anger radiated from her like a lethal poison.

Caelum and Nero stepped in line with Draven. The griffin's golden eyes, usually filled with mischief, were now narrow slits of suspicion. "She's still blocking me," Caelum whispered, his voice audible over the echoing footsteps.

"She's pissed." Draven glanced at Caelum, his brow furrowing. "I guess I can't blame her. I acted on impulse and emotion and spilled our secret."

Draven's gaze shifted to the griffin next to him. Nero's gaze was locked on Lanae as she walked a half a block ahead of them. Normally, when they were out, his preference was to walk with Lanae, not him and Caelum. His usual open and mischievous eyes were narrowed, his ears pinned back against his head. His nails clicked on the cobblestone, a sharp, rhythmic sound that added to the tension.

"That wasn't your finest moment, but at least they know," Caelum said.

Draven sighed, his irrational actions pressing down on him. "The last time she didn't heed the council's directives, she was tried for treason." He slashed his gaze to Caelum, the memory of that debacle still fresh and painful.

Caelum nodded, his expression grim. "The last time, there were some members controlled by Xoltan Firetwill."

Draven grunted an acknowledgment as they rounded the corner to their street. The familiar sight of their house should have been comforting, but Lanae walked right past it, her mind clearly elsewhere.

"Where are you going?" Draven called as he stopped at the walkway leading to their place. Caelum and Nero headed inside, their footsteps fading into the background.

Lanae turned, her eyes darting around before she backtracked to the house. She bypassed Draven without a word, her face a mask of frustration and distraction. The minute he closed the door, she spoke, her voice sharp and accusatory.

"You interrupted the meeting before we could settle on a plan." Her gaze bore into him, hard and unyielding.

He cocked his head, studying her. "That's why you are mad?"

"Yes. Why else would I be?" she snapped, her tone defensive.

Draven glanced over her head at Caelum and then met her gaze. Something unsettling gnawed at him. "No reason." His skin prickled with unease.

Nero squawked from the kitchen, pulling her attention away. "What is that thing doing inside?" she demanded, her voice tinged with disdain.

Draven couldn't believe those words tumbled out of his wife's mouth. Hell, he no longer believed this was his wife. There was only one sure way to find out. He reached for her and wrapped his fingers around her wrist. The expected tingling sensation of their bond was absent. No electric connection sparked between them. He narrowed his gaze, suspicion turning to certainty. "You are not Lanae," he growled.

She twisted her wrist and moved her arm down, breaking free of his grip with a fluid motion. Then she spun around him and delivered a swift kick to his lower back, sending him off-balance. He stumbled, catching himself on the couch, but by the time he reached the front door, she was gone, with only the echo of her footsteps and the lingering sense of alarm in her wake.

MOVEMENT OUTSIDE HER CAGE jerked Lanae from her stupor, and she lifted her gaze. The cold iron bars prevented her from leaning closer. Shadows danced under the dusky haze outside her cage. Her heart stuttered at the green eyes studying her from the other side of the bars. A flicker of hope ignited within her, pushing back the despair that had settled in her chest. She shot to her feet. "Draven."

"Hello, love. It's time we get you out of there. Don't you think?"

His voice soothed her frazzled nerves, and for a moment, the damp, musty air of the cage seemed to lift.

Lanae's heart soared and she stepped forward, reaching through the bars for him, but he moved away. The lack of contact left her fingers tingling with a desperate longing.

A key turning in the lock caught her attention, the metallic click echoing through the stone chamber. She glanced at the metal positioned in the lock, blinking in surprise. "How did you get the key?"

"I found Granger and beat it out of him." His eyes glinted with a hint of satisfaction. He opened the door, using it as a barrier between them before he spun on his heels and headed toward the hallway. "This way."

A gnawing itch surfaced in Lanae's mind, but she was not about to complain about his no-nonsense attitude. She followed him down the stairwell and into the dungeons without question. The air grew colder, the stink of mold intensifying with each step. When he stepped into an open cell, she hesitated, her instincts screaming at her to be cautious.

"Draven?" she called. Her voice held the slightest of trembles.

He glanced over his shoulder at her and smiled, though it lacked its usual warmth. "The exit is hidden somewhere over here." He ran his hand over the rough stone wall. "Come help me find the lever to open it."

Alarms sounded in her head, but she stepped to the wall next to him, running her hands over the cold, uneven surface. As her fingers got close to his, he snapped an iron cuff around her wrist. The metal bit into her skin, and she cried out, blinking at the iron singeing her wrist and then up into those familiar green eyes.

His hand grasped her throat with a vise-like grip, pressing her against the wall.

The cold stone sent racking quakes down her spine, and she blinked at his feral sneer, her brain clearing enough to note that there was no tingling from his touch. "You aren't Draven."

"Funny, your husband said the same thing earlier." His voice dripped with malice as he pressed his body against hers, pinning her to the wall.

The stench of sweat and decay filled her nostrils, making her gag.

She swung with her free hand, but as swift as a lightning bolt, that wrist was bound in iron as well. The cuffs burned against her skin, leaving angry red welts.

When her captor stepped back, his form altered, shifting from Draven to her own image, to Granger, and then to eyes that were frighteningly familiar. His nearly black eyes stared at her with the same contempt as Xoltan had. Although this fae's form was more muscular and powerful than Xoltan's. His hair shone bright with a weave of silver and white threaded with midnight, and his complexion was a pleasant golden tan, as if he spent days in the tropics. If she had been single and this was a bar, this fiend would have caught her attention.

His lips twerked into a grin, and he glanced around the dungeon with an air of disdain. "This is a much better place for you than on display in the main hall."

Rage flared within her, and she kicked out, her foot connecting with his shin. The impact sent a jolt of satisfaction through her, but it was short-lived.

He struck as quickly as a snake, his palm leaving a sting so hot on her cheek that her vision blurred with bright lights from the impact. The force of the blow made her ears ring, and she fought to stay conscious, her heart gunned into overdrive as she faced the twisted fae before her.

"Who the fuck are you?" she demanded, her voice trembling as adrenaline pumped her muscles full of fury. The dank air of the dungeon closed in around her, amplifying her sense of urgency.

"Allow me to introduce myself. Spric Firetwill. Shapeshifter extraordinaire." He bowed with a flourish, his movement fluid and almost graceful, close enough to tempt her. The dim light glinted off his hair, casting an eerie glow on his features.

She kicked out again, her foot slicing through the air, nearly connecting with his face.

He jerked back just in time. His sudden motion sent a surge of satisfaction through her. His hands balled into fists, and his gaze darkened, becoming a storm of malevolent intent.

She braced herself; her heart jackhammered in her chest, and she parried the incoming swing with a desperate burst of strength.

She deflected his first hit, but the second landed squarely in her abdomen. The impact was like a sledgehammer, yanking all the air from her lungs and doubling her over. Pain radiated through her torso, and she gasped, fighting to stay upright.

He stepped out of reach, his breath coming in heavy huffs, his anger drilling into her as hard as his fist had. The air crackled with tension. He grabbed her face with a rough hand, his grip bruising, and tilted it up, forcing her to meet his gaze. "While I would love to spar with you and see what type of damage you could do, this is my domain, and you will show me some respect. Especially since your life is in my hands." His low, dangerous growl crusted ice over her backbone.

She spit at him, her defiance unfiltered, and received a backhand to the same cheek. The force of the blow sent her reeling, knocking her to the ground. Her cheek throbbed with pain, and her vision blurred with tears. The cold, hard stone bit into her skin as she lay there, struggling to regain her bearings. The tang of blood filled her mouth, reminding her of her vulnerability.

The dungeon's oppressive silence closed in around her, broken only by the rasp of his heavy breathing and her own ragged gasps. She forced herself to look up at him, her eyes blazing with defiance. She knew she couldn't afford to show any weakness, not now, not in front of him.

"Respect?" She spit a wad of blood on the floor, the metallic taste lingering on her tongue. "You'll never have my respect." Her voice was insolent, though her body trembled from the pain and exhaustion. The stone floor beneath her seemed like ice against her skin, and the dim light cast eerie shadows on the damp, moss-covered walls.

He smiled with a calculated expression that jellied her spine. "Then I'll have your life." His words dripped with menace, and the surrounding air seemed to grow colder, amplifying the dread settling in her chest.

An artic chill started in her stomach and spiraled outward, sending goose bumps up her arms and down her spine. She tried to mask her fear, willing her muscles to stay steady, but the way his smile widened, she knew he saw the brief flash of terror in her eyes. The air suddenly thickened, and her heart beat against her sternum like a drum.

"After some much deserved torture, of course." His words dripped with sinister delight, echoing off the stone walls.

He turned and left her lying on the cold, damp floor, the pain of his fists still fresh and throbbing in her body. Mold and decay filled her nostrils, and his receding footsteps reverberated in the eerie silence, leaving her alone in the darkness with her fear.

# CHAPTER SIX
## *Ties of Blood*

DRAVEN RAN BOTH HANDS into his hair as he paced their living room. The soft glow of the lanterns cast long shadows on the walls, adding to the oppressive atmosphere. "What in the ever-loving afterlife was that?" he exclaimed, his desperation and confusion ringing through the room.

Caelum blinked incessantly, his eyes narrowing in concentration as he tried to telepathically reach his sister. The strain caused his temples to pound, and the silence in his mind was maddening. Not a damn thing was coming through, and he was just as frantic as Draven. A sudden thought jerked his head up, and his eyes widened with realization. "Granger."

Draven spun toward him, his movements abrupt. "What?"

"We need to speak to Granger. They said he never showed for work. Maybe he saw that thing's actual face." Caelum's voice was filled with urgency as he headed for the door, still dressed in his uniform.

Draven followed without hesitation, his steps echoing loudly in the quiet room. He put his hand up at Nero, who was watching with anxious eyes. "If she comes back, have her let you out and find us. Okay?"

Nero nodded, his feathers rustling softly.

Caelum waited impatiently for Draven to lock the door before he headed to the neighborhood of upscale homes near the Citadel where the elite officers lived. The frosty night air bit into their exposed skin, and the cobblestones beneath their feet seemed to reflect the tension in the air.

The minute they stepped into the neighborhood, the sound of a commotion drew their attention. A gaggle of guards were milling about, their voices raised in anger. A hulking figure threw a punch at another guard, the impact resonating with a sickening thud. His rambling curses reached Caelum's ears, and even under the shadowy glow, he could see the bruise on the fighting man's temple.

Granger yelled he did not desert his post, his voice a mix of anger and desperation. The surrounding guards were clearly trying to arrest the poor bastard, their grips tight on their weapons.

Caelum jumped into a sprint, his heart pumping a ragged breath. He had to intercept before they arrested Granger. The cool night air whipped against his face, and the uneven cobblestones threatened to trip him, but he pushed on, determined to reach Granger in time.

"Wait!" His call distracted the guards and Granger, halting their struggles. The chilly night air seemed to grow still as all eyes locked on Caelum, and Draven trailing him. The distant sounds of the city were a faint murmur, overshadowed by the tension crackling in the air.

As Caelum approached with his palms out in supplication, one of the arresting guards snarled at him, his face contorted with irritation. "This is none of your concern, newbie." The guard's breath was visible in the chilly air, adding to the harshness of his words.

Beating other officers was highly frowned upon by the guard, even during an arrest. Caelum pointed at the blue and purple bruise marring Granger's face. "Clearly Granger was knocked unconscious, unless you caused that fucking bruise." He expected the guards to recoil.

And recoil they did. It was as if Caelum's words had knocked some sense into these men. The tension in their stances eased. "No. He had that when we arrived," the lead guard said, his tone defensive.

The man's name embroidered on his uniform was faded, but Caelum squinted at it until he could make it out—Kale.

"Look, Kale," Caelum continued, his voice urgent, "Jenna said Granger came to escort my sister to the situation room."

Granger growled, his eyes dark with frustration. "I did no such thing."

Caelum put his hand up to calm him. "I know. But someone wearing your face did. Just like someone wearing my sister's face infiltrated the situation room meeting that we interrupted. The person who came back to our house was not my sister."

Skepticism blanketed the group. The guards exchanged dubious glances, and even Granger crossed his arms, his brow furrowed in doubt.

"How do you know?" Kale asked, his gaze piercing.

"Because I know my wife. And that was not her," Draven growled, his conviction clear.

Caelum let his eyes drift shut, and he huffed a breath. "You all know I have a telepathic connection with Lanae." When he opened his eyes, everyone was nodding. "I could not telepathically reach her, even when she was in our home and in front of me. I didn't even feel her blocking me out. That's how I knew it wasn't her."

"And Nero wouldn't go near her," Draven added.

At the mention of the griffin, the guards straightened and dropped their tight-armed stance. They had seen the bond between Nero and Lanae out on the training fields over the last three years. "Nero doesn't leave her side," one of the other soldiers said, his voice laced with respect.

"No. He doesn't unless she forces him to," Caelum replied, his eyes meeting each guard in turn.

"Maybe he was upset with her for stopping his storm antics this morning," one officer suggested, trying to rationalize the situation.

"Have you ever seen that griffin turn a cold shoulder on Lanae?" Caelum challenged.

They all grumbled and shook their heads, acknowledging the truth in his words.

Caelum met Granger's gaze, his expression earnest. "I am hoping you can tell me what the person who did that to you looked like." He pointed at the bruise on Granger's face.

Granger's eyes darkened with the memory. "I was blindsided. The only thing I saw was a pair of upscale steel-toe boots and a black duster coat before darkness claimed me. And then I woke up in my own bed and I couldn't find my uniform." He looked at the officers surrounding him with his frustration on full display. "And then these buffoons showed up."

The cold air blanketed them, the reality of their situation sinking in. They had a shape-shifting enemy among them, and the stakes had never been higher.

DRAVEN'S PULSE POUNDED IN his temples like a roar of an avalanche, echoing with relentless intensity. The arguments still raged between the guards, creating a whirlwind of frantic energy, the air thick with the metallic tang of tension. His one relief was that the council and generals had not settled on a course of action before his and Caelum's interruption.

Whoever had been impersonating Granger and Lanae hadn't gotten the vital information on the pending battle tactics. Their deception was foiled in the chaos.

He grabbed Caelum's arm, his fingers gripping with urgency, pulling him away from the guards who were now bickering heatedly, their voices a commotion of discord over what to do with the newfound information and Granger's orchestrated desertion. "Caelum, I need to go find Lanae," Draven said, his voice low but vibrating with intensity.

"I'm going with you," Caelum replied, his eyes dark with determination.

"No. You need to stay here and make sure the shit doesn't hit the fan. If my hunch is right…" Draven's voice trailed off as he mopped the sweat from his face, the salt stinging his eyes.

"You needed me last time," Caelum insisted, his gaze unwavering.

"If she is there, she's not there for breeding." The word hissed from between Draven's lips like a curse. "She's there because they think she killed Xoltan."

Caelum blinked, the reality of Draven's words sinking in, then closed his eyes. The heavy truth hung between them, thick as the fog that shrouded Solstice City. Few knew Draven had been the true savior. Outside of Faide and Varkir, no one else knew besides Caelum. Lanae had been revered as their liberator. "Fuck."

"That's usually my line," Draven muttered, a sardonic edge to his voice.

Caelum's lips twitched into a wry smile. "I am going with you," he repeated, his voice firmer.

"No. You are not. You are going to make sure your parents stay safe. If Alestain is there, he will reanimate his brother's minions. He needs an army before he attacks."

"How are you even going to get there? You destroyed the only portal to that realm."

Draven met his gaze, his eyes burning with resolve. "With another ancient draconian spell."

Caelum lifted an eyebrow, skepticism mingling with curiosity. He crossed his arms, the leather of his tunic creaking. "You mean you not only know how to destroy portals, you know how to open them?"

Draven smirked, the expression a fleeting glimpse of his confidence. "How do you think I got inside these walls to begin with?" He glanced around, ensuring no one was eavesdropping on their tense exchange.

Caelum wiped the perspiration from his face, conscious of the grit from the day's battles.

"You also have to go tell the council that the person in the war room was not Lanae. That is just as important as making sure your parents stay put." Draven tapped Caelum's chest, the gesture both reassuring and commanding.

"Fine. But I'll need more than my word after the shitshow earlier." Caelum glanced at the group of soldiers still arguing, then crossed to Granger.

Draven didn't wait to see what Caelum said to the elite guard. He slipped through the shadows, his steps quick and silent as he went in search of a secluded alley where he could perform his spell.

LANAE BANGED THE BACK of her head against the cold, unforgiving stone wall in frustration, the dull thud reverberating in the dank, confined space. The cell walls seemed to shrink, the oppressive darkness highlighting her inability to break free from the heavy chains around her wrists. Her abdomen still ached where Spric had punched her...a deep, throbbing pain that wouldn't let her forget the assault. Her stomach growled its gnawing emptiness, and she wondered just how long she would be deprived of food.

The iron door to the dungeons creaked open, the sound echoing through the narrow corridors. She held her breath, her pulse quickening. When Draven stepped in front of the cage, her heart stuttered, a moment of hope flaring before being crushed. The lack of weapons hanging on his belt and the keys in his hand told her this wasn't her sweet dragon. This was an imposter, a cruel mimicry.

He grinned a twisted smile that made her nerves jitter through her muscles in a flight response. He slid the key in the lock and turned it before he swung the door open; the hinges groaned in protest. He stepped inside, the dim light casting ominous shadows across his face.

"Stop with the mind fuck." Her voice remained steady despite the terror clawing at her insides. She scrambled to her feet, the chains rattling with her movement.

His laughter bounced off the rock walls, a chilling sound that seemed to mock her defiance. He stepped closer, the air swirling heavy with menace.

She shifted into ready form, muscles tensing, and waited. Her reach wasn't far, but if he came into her sphere, she'd try her damnedest to land a hit. He moved to the outer edge of where the chains halted her punch, a deliberate taunt. The wicked gleam in his eyes was enough to send a bolt of fear through her, icy and paralyzing.

"It's time to face my father." His voice crawled in a low, menacing growl. He inched closer, the dim light casting a sinister shadow across his face.

Lanae swung with all her might, her fist slicing through the musty air.

The bastard's reflexes were lightning-fast. He caught her fist with a sharp, audible snap, his grip like iron. In one swift motion, he twisted her arm behind her back. Her joints protested with a sickening crack. With a brutal force, he slammed her into the back wall face-first. The impact reverberated through her skull, a dull thud echoing in the confined space. The cold, rough stone scraped against her cheek, and blood filled her mouth as she bit down on her lip.

He pressed against her, the weight of his body pinning her to the cold, unyielding wall. The clinging dampness of the cell enveloped them. "Besides, I enjoy messing with murderers," he sneered, his breath hot against her ear.

With a surge of defiance, Lanae slammed her head back. The satisfying crunch of bone meeting bone echoed through the confined space as she connected with his face. He grunted, a guttural sound of pain and surprise, and cursed under his breath, his grip momentarily loosening.

He moved his free hand to grip her throat hard enough to cut off her air. "If you keep this up, you will be more than just bloodied and bruised."

"Fuck you." She hissed out the curse from what little air she could get.

"Is that what you want?" He pressed his pelvis against her, and she stilled at the feel of his hard length pressing into the small of her back. "Because I think I have time to oblige."

He tightened the chain on her shackles, forcing her hands to pin to the wall.

The minute his hand removed from her throat, she gasped for breath, the precious air filling her lungs. Desperation clawed at her insides, and she screamed, "No!" Her voice echoed through the cold stone walls, a haunting cry of defiance.

He released the chains, the metallic clinking sound reverberating in the silence. "Then be a good girl and put both hands behind your back," he commanded, his voice dripping with sinister intent.

Lanae inched her trembling hands behind her back, the cold shackles biting into her skin. She hated the fear lashing her form, the icy tendrils wrapping around her heart. She could deal with the physical pain, the bruises and blood, but the thought of something more vile sent waves of dread crashing over her.

Another set of manacles clamped around her wrists before the ones connected to the walls clattered to the ground. He spun her around with a rough jerk, forcing her to face him. The bastard still wore Draven's form, a twisted mockery of her beloved. Anger surged within her, and she kicked his shin with all her might. The illusion of Draven wavered like a mirage.

He snarled and grabbed a handful of her hair, yanking her head back painfully. His cloying scent, a sickening blend of sweat and decay, filled her nose, making her stomach churn. "I will cut off your foot if you kick me again," he threatened, his voice a venomous hiss.

"Drop the façade," she commanded, her voice steady despite the turmoil roiling inside her.

He chuckled, a dark, sinister sound that reverberated through the cold, damp air. "I don't think so. What better way to screw with your mind than having the image of your husband beat you to within an inch of your life?" His eyes glittered with cruel amusement as he spoke.

She swallowed hard, her throat dry and constricted. The metallic tingle of fear lingered on her tongue as he yanked her forward with a vicious tug. The rough stone floor slid against her feet, and the cold, oppressive air pressed in around her, heightening her sense of helplessness.

He gripped her arm with an ironclad hold, his fingers digging painfully into her flesh as he dragged her up the winding staircase. Each step echoed ominously in the narrow corridor, the sound amplifying her sense of dread. The air grew colder the higher they ascended, and Lanae's heart hammered in her chest like a steady pulse of thunder.

When they crossed into the throne room, the sudden shift in atmosphere was almost suffocating. Lanae shivered involuntarily at the view of the immaculate marble floor and the gleaming dais. The room was eerily pristine, every surface polished to perfection, erasing any trace of the carnage that had unfolded here three years prior. The contrast was jarring, a cruel mockery of the memories that haunted her.

Yet no amount of cleanliness could wipe away the horrors embedded in her mind. Rorik's dying screams echoed hauntingly in her ears, a ghostly chorus that resonated with her deepest fears. She could almost see the blood that had pooled on the floor, feel the oppressive weight of despair that had filled the room. The raw anguish of that moment crashed over her like a tidal wave, threatening to drown her in sorrow.

A man with hair as white as Rorik's stood with his back to them, his posture rigid and alert. The dim light of the chamber cast long shadows across his form. When he turned, the faint glint of light illuminated his face. A face that, if he had black hair, would have mirrored that of his brother. The one Draven had shown her in his memory. But what struck her more than the face from Draven's past was the heart-shaped crystal that was sewn into his chest plate. The Dragon's Heart. Except now it did not hold that vibrant red color she had seen in Draven's memories, as if all the power in the stone had been used and all that was left was an empty shell.

His gaze fell on the form Spric wore. His face blanched, the color draining away as though he had seen a ghost. He took an involuntary step back, his heel hitting the cold, unforgiving glass behind him with a sharp, echoing clink. Fear flashed over his features, contorting them momentarily into a mask of terror. "Viserion?" he asked in a whisper, his voice quivering with dread.

The illusion of Draven faltered before dissolving completely, leaving Spric standing in his true form. He cocked his head at his father, a curious glint in his eyes. "Who is Viserion?" His voice carried a note of genuine confusion.

Alestain's face twisted with anger, his eyes narrowing into slits. His voice rose, echoing off the marble walls. "Why the hell would you wear the illusion of the dragon king in front of me?" he demanded, the words laced with a mixture of fury and incredulity. The tension in the air was palpable, a charged silence settling between them.

"I wore the illusion of her husband, not the dragon king." With a brutal shove, he pushed Lanae forward, the force sending her sprawling to her knees.

The rough stone floor scraped against her skin, tearing at her clothing. She winced at the pain, but kept her eyes fixed on the man in front of her.

Alestain's face twisted with rage, his eyes burning with a fierce intensity. "You dare mock me with such trickery?" His thunderous roar echoed through the chamber. He took a step forward, his presence menacing, but Spric remained unperturbed, a smirk playing on his lips.

Lanae's heart ricocheted in her ribs, each beat a painful sign of her vulnerability. The memories of her captivity and the torment she endured flooded her mind, but she forced herself to focus, to find a way out of this hellhole.

Spric's eyes gleamed with malice as he turned to Alestain. "You misunderstand, Father. It's not mockery. It's a lesson." He reached down, grabbing Lanae's chin and forcing her to look up at him. "A lesson in justice."

Alestain's expression shifted, a flicker of uncertainty crossing his features. He glanced at Lanae. "What lesson?"

Spric's grip tightened, his fingers digging into her skin like iron claws. "The lesson that no one is beyond the law," he snarled at her before meeting his father's gaze.

A tremor ran down Lanae's spine at his words, a shiver of dread that she couldn't suppress. She could see the twisted satisfaction in Spric's eyes, the malevolent gleam that revealed how much he enjoyed her suffering. The room shrank around her, the air saturated with the scent of damp stone and fear. But she refused to break. Gritting her teeth, she summoned her strength, preparing for whatever came next. Her heart went on a spree, drumming a rapid beat in her ears.

"What fucking law?" she spat, the words slipping out in a fiery outburst of defiance. Her voice echoed sharply in the confined space.

"You killed a king," Alestain snapped, his tone harsh and accusatory, reverberating off the cold stone walls. A damning indictment that only deepened the oppressive atmosphere.

"A king who exiled you for killing all the dragons." Every syllable was tinged with quiet defiance. She didn't deny killing Xoltan because that would implicate Draven, and her protective instincts were far stronger than her sense of self-preservation. Her eyes, intense and unyielding, bore into Alestain's with a fierceness that mirrored the storm brewing outside. "Which clearly wasn't the case."

Alestain blinked several times, the flickering torchlight casting shifting shadows across his face, before his eyes narrowed into sharp, probing slits. "You are the wife of the new dragon king?" His voice was low, almost a growl, filled with distrust.

"There is no dragon king. Solstice City is run by the Fae Council. We are not a monarchy like we once were centuries ago." Her voice held a quiet strength, unwavering despite the tension crackling in the room like a taut bowstring.

"Well, that will certainly change once I am through with it." He speared his son with a glare as cold and unrelenting as a winter's night. "Her pretty head on a pike will make a gory statement at the head of our army, don't you think?"

Spric's face drained of color, the blood visibly retreating, leaving him pale and wide-eyed. "Uh, sure?" His grip on her face loosened with a minor tremble.

It seemed like her captor might love to use his fists, but the idea of killing didn't seem to sit well with the young shapeshifter. The scent of sweat and fear permeated the room, mingling with the aroma of the stone walls.

"Once I awaken the army, we will deal with the murderess. Let her rot in the dungeon until it's time for her to meet her maker." The words were accompanied by a dismissive wave, his back already turned to them as he gazed out of the window at the twilight sky, lost in his own grim thoughts. The distant laments and howls of the wind outside seemed to echo the cold finality of his decree.

LANAE'S FOOTSTEPS ECHOED SOFTLY in the narrow stone stairwell, the air thick with the indication of earth. The flickering torchlight cast long shadows on the ancient walls, creating an eerie atmosphere. The silence stretched between them until they descended.

"You're not a killer, are you?" Her voice was audible over the creak of each wooden step.

"Shut up," he snarled, his tone dark and cutting like the blade he always kept by his side.

"Have you ever fought in a war?" She pressed on, her eyes narrowing as she sought the chinks in his armor. She could sense his unease, his reluctance to relive those memories. The scent of sweat and leather mingled with the cold air surrounding them.

"If you don't shut up, I will throw you down the staircase," he threatened, his eyes burning with a fierce determination, though his hands trembled just the slightest bit.

She fell silent, allowing the tension to build. The only sound was the rhythmic thud of their boots on the wooden steps. "Taking a life is not easy," she finally said in the confined space.

He halted, his breath hot and ragged against her face as he slammed her back into the rough stone wall, the impact resonating through her bones. He loomed over her, his body a wall of seething anger and muscle.

"I have never been a soldier during wartime. I've never had to kill," he growled, his voice a low, dangerous rumble that reverberated in the pit of her stomach, but his words confirmed her suspicion.

She met his gaze with a calm, soft understanding instead of defiance. "I never took it lightly." Her voice was soft and steady despite the closeness of his threatening presence. The sincerity in her eyes seemed to reach him, and he hesitated, the hard lines of his face softening for a fleeting moment.

"Then you will understand why I will have to do what I am ordered to when the time comes," he muttered, the fire in his eyes dimming into a smoldering ember.

"I've only killed when my life was on the line. I never sought to deliver death. And I've chosen not to kill someone I viewed as an enemy." Her words hung in the cold, damp air between them, filled with the sincerity of her conviction. The chill nipped at her skin, a pronounced difference to the heat of the confrontation.

He stared at her, his gaze piercing, as if her words were chipping away at his will. His breath was a mix of frustration and uncertainty swirling in the limited space they shared. He stepped back, giving her a few inches of breathing room, but the tension remained intense. "How was your life on the line with my uncle?"

"He had a sword to my throat," she replied, the memory causing a slight tremor in her voice.

His gaze dropped to her throat, inspecting it for any signs of injury. The torchlight flickered, throwing shadows that danced across her skin. He scoffed and crossed his arms, his skepticism clear. The aroma of leather and iron saturated the air, blending with a subtle hint of fear.

Lanae gulped down a steadying breath, her chest rising and falling in a measured rhythm.

She closed her eyes and summoned an illusion of her bolting down the stairs, the echoes of phantom footsteps and the imagined swish of her hair trailing behind her. The sound was convincing, reverberating through the stairwell.

Spric's eyes widened, and he immediately ran after the illusion, his heavy boots pounding on the wooden steps.

Lanae opened her eyes and took another breath, creeping up the stairs to the landing they had passed moments before. Each step was deliberate, the wood creaking softly under her weight. Her heart clanged in her chest, but she maintained her calm.

She turned the knob with a slow, careful twist and cringed at the slight creak it made. The illusion below held strong. The echoes of Spric's ranting about what he would do if he caught her filled the air, masking her movements. The door opened, revealing a dark hallway. She stepped into the shadows, her movements as silent as the night itself, and shut the door with the same stealth.

Leaning against the cold stone wall, she allowed herself a moment of respite, her breathing shallow and controlled. She then squatted as low to the ground as she could, her muscles tensing and protesting the position. Slowly, she threaded one ankle through her bound wrists and then the other. The iron cuffs bit into her skin, but she ignored the pain.

She stood and let out a breath, her hands now in front of her. She flexed her fingers and the warmth of returning circulation tingled through each appendage. With her hands freed, a surge of confidence filled her. She was ready to defend herself if needed. She silently thanked the gods above for twilight, this near to a full moon, knowing this was the time her powers were close to their strongest. Even these iron cuffs couldn't douse her power of illusion. If he had gotten her back in that cell, it would have been another story entirely.

Her eyes slowly adjusted to the murky shadows that cloaked the hallway. The air was cool and musty, carrying the scent of aged wood and long-forgotten secrets. She crept toward the first door, her heartbeat echoing in her ears. Testing the knob, the smooth, cold metal pressed against her skin. It turned easily, and she slid into the room, her breath shallow with anticipation. She hoped to find a weapon or something to pick the lock on her shackles.

The candles flickered, casting jittery, elongated shadows that danced on the walls. She paused, her eyes widening at the expansive laboratory before her. The space was eerily still, the silence almost deafening. Figures stood motionless at each workstation, lifeless yet ominously poised for reanimation. The flickering candlelight gave them a ghostly appearance, their shadows stretching grotesquely across the room.

Lanae moved cautiously through the labyrinth of tables, her footsteps a whisper on the cold stone floor. The air filled with burning wax and faint chemical scents. She glanced at the carvings etched into the side of each table, deciphering the intricate inscriptions that explained each workstation. Her eyes flitted from one word to another until they landed on "portals."

Her gaze shifted to the capped vials lining the table. There had to be a hundred neat green vials, arranged meticulously in rows of ten. The glass gleamed faintly, the liquid inside shimmering with a mysterious allure.

She reached for them, her fingers brushing against the cool glass. The room suddenly came alive with the sound of rustling fabric and the creak of ancient joints. As if on cue, the figures in the room started to move all at once.

# CHAPTER SEVEN
## *Parental Struggles*

TWILIGHT PAINTED THE SKY the color of the pink highlights in Lanae's hair, the hues blending with the soft lavender and deepening indigo of the evening. Draven took a breath, calming his jumbled nerves, the crisp night air filling his lungs and grounding him in the present.

"Focus," he whispered, his breath forming a misty cloud in the cooling air. The key to opening portals was homing in on where you wanted it to drop you before you cast the spell. He did not want to be dropped right in the middle of the throne room. If Alestain was there and had reanimated the army, that would be a dangerous place to appear. Same with showing up where they destroyed the mind machine.

His thoughts jumped to the room where he found Caelum in a compromising position. The memory brought a slight flush to his cheeks, but it was a safer place to materialize than either of the other rooms that held disturbing memories.

He uttered the spell in the guttural language of his kin, the ancient words rumbling through his chest, and the air churned like a rising storm. The draconian words took no time to open a vortex between worlds before him. He stepped through it without the usual tug and tumble of a normal portal. This was more like stepping from one room to another, or over a threshold of a house, the transition smooth and seamless.

The minute both his feet touched down on the cool obsidian floor, the portal hissed out of existence behind him. He stared at the ashes at the foot of the bed, the remnants of what once was a figure now a scattered, fragile dust. Time had knocked the ash-formed figure into a delicate pile. Nothing in the room had changed, not even the discarded clothing on the floor. The air was stale, carrying a faint scent of decay and old fabric.

He picked up the shirt and the skirt, the fabric rough and brittle in his hands, and tossed them over the conspicuous pile, covering it from view. He chewed on his lip, the motion mingling with his thoughts, and glanced at the bedroom door, wondering whether the halls were safe.

He stepped toward the door, his boots barely making a sound on the hard floor. The sudden noise in the hall had him backing up quickly. His heart whirred in pace with a galloping horse's hoofbeats. He scanned the room, his eyes darting to every shadow. When his gaze landed on the wardrobe, he moved, slipping inside as stealthy as a ghost, the wood creaking under his weight. The bedroom door opened, and then someone yelled, "Clear!" before slamming it shut again.

Draven let out a breath he didn't realize he was holding, the tension draining from his body. He sagged on the back wall, which shifted with a soft click, revealing a hidden path through the walls. He nearly laughed, remembering the secret passages in their castle long ago. The memory brought a brief smile to his lips.

He slid inside the narrow passage, the walls pressing close against his shoulders. He sucked in his stomach and shuffled through the tight space, the stone walls cool and rough against his skin.

A familiar voice boomed, stopping him in his tracks. The sound reverberated through the cold stone walls, sending a quiver tripping up his back.

"I am Alestain Firetwill. You now bow to me." The voice was deep and authoritative, filling the cavernous space with its oppressive weight.

Cold fury gripped Draven, his muscles tensing like coiled springs. He squeezed his eyes shut and fisted his hands, the rough texture of the worn leather gloves biting into his palms. He couldn't light this place on fire with the possibility of Lanae being here. As much as he wanted to raze this castle and reclaim the Dragon's Heart, he had to find her first.

After a moment, a chorus of voices replied, "Yes, master." Their unified response echoed eerily, like a dissonant symphony in the vast chamber.

"I want this castle cleaned and polished until it shines."

"Yes, master."

"Find my son and bring the prisoner up from the dungeon. It's time to enact justice for my brother's death." The command was filled with icy determination, each word cutting and precise.

The patter of running feet leaving the throne room echoed through the tight space, bouncing off the ancient stone walls. Draven moved with purpose, his footsteps light and swift. A cool draft filtered through the narrow corridor, carrying with it a bouquet of mildew and decay.

He moved until he found a staircase, the worn steps descending into darkness. The flickering torchlight cast elongated shadows that danced eerily on the walls. The air grew colder as he descended; the chill seeped through his clothes and bit at his skin. He had to get to Lanae before the minions did.

LANAE'S FINGERS TREMBLED AS she grabbed a handful of the green vials, their glass surfaces cool and smooth against her skin. With a sweeping motion, she knocked the remaining vials to the floor. The sound of shattering glass echoed around the room, a chaotic symphony as dozens of portals tore open, distorting the air with a shimmering iridescence.

She staggered back, her vision momentarily obscured by the swirling vortexes that blocked her view of the people reanimating in the room. Her heart pounded wildly in her chest, each beat a drum of urgency as she darted toward a door at the back. The vials clinked together as she slid them into her shirt, keeping one gripped tightly in her hand.

The hallway buzzed around her, the faint hum of arcane energy vibrating through the walls. She thought of home, the image of safety and warmth flickering in her mind as she tossed the vial to the ground. A brilliant flash of light erupted as the portal opened.

Spric's thunderous footsteps echoed as he barreled down the hall after her.

She dove through the gateway, tasting the sweetness of freedom as the sensation of space bending gripped her. She plopped on the hardwood floor of her home's entryway in Solstice City. Her relief was cut short as Spric crashed down on top of her, his eyes wild with fury.

"Oh, no you don't." His breath hissed in her ear.

One vial freed from her shirt and rolled on the hardwood as she scrambled to get away, her breath coming in ragged gasps.

Nero's squawking roar tore through the air, jerking both their heads up. A bolt of lightning split the room, its bright light momentarily blinding.

Spric threw himself off her, narrowly avoiding the electrifying strike. He swiped the vial off the ground and bolted out of the house, leaving Lanae heaving on the floor, her limbs trembling with adrenaline.

Nero turned and disappeared into the open door of her parents' bedroom with the same urgency as he had chased Spric with.

Lanae's chest cramped with the triple overdrive her heart jumped into. *Alestain had reanimated his minions.* Which meant her parents were awake. She jumped to her feet and slid into the room, her breath hitching at the scene before her.

Her father had his hands around Caelum's throat, his grip merciless. Her mother, frantic, was throwing belongings into a bag as if packing for a long trip.

"Let him go!" Lanae's cry rang through the room, mingling with the sharp, crackling sounds of lightning from Nero.

One bolt connected with her mother, causing her to stiffen; a small wisp of black smoke escaped her lips. Desperation surged through Lanae as she grabbed her father, trying to wrench him off Caelum. Caelum's face was turning an alarming shade of blue from lack of oxygen.

"Lanae?" Her mother met her gaze, a plea etched into her features.

"Tell Dad to stop choking Caelum!" Lanae cried, her voice breaking.

Her mother moved quickly, snatching a vase from the table and smashing it against her father's head. He crumpled to the floor, unconscious.

The vacant look of those under mind control returned to her mother's eyes. But before she could retaliate against them, Lanae grabbed Caelum, his limp body heavy against her, and with Nero by her side, she dragged him into the hall and locked the door behind them.

Caelum gasped for breath, his chest heaving as he curled into a ball, tears streaming down his face.

*I'm here.* Lanae sent the thought, her heart aching with a deep, resonating pain. He moved closer, hugging her with a tight grip, his form trembling violently with sobs that racked his entire body. She brought her chained hands over his head, the cold metal links pressing against the back of his tunic, and held him close as the severity of the chaos that had just unfolded settled heavily on her shoulders.

"They didn't even recognize me," he sobbed, his voice breaking, each word a dagger to her heart.

"You were seven when they were taken. You've grown quite a bit since then." Her voice was gentle yet tinged with an underlying sorrow.

He nodded, but kept his arms around her, his grip tightening as if she were the only thing anchoring him to reality, keeping him from shattering into pieces.

"Where's Draven?" she asked when her breathing returned to normal and Caelum's sobs had subsided into soft, hiccupping breaths. The warmth of his tears soaked into her shirt.

Caelum pulled away slowly, and she moved her arms from around him, the chains clinking softly. He stared at the iron bindings on her wrists, his brow furrowing in concern, and wiped his face free of tear tracks. "He went to find you."

Caelum lifted his hand and touched her face, his fingers gentle and warm against her bruised skin. She winced at the contact and instinctively recoiled, the pain flaring sharply. She could only imagine what she looked like after the brutal beating Spric had given her—the swelling, the darkening bruises, the cuts that still oozed blood.

His words were slow to register, her mind foggy now that the last remnants of adrenaline had been exhausted. But when they finally sank in, her stomach plummeted, a heavy, nauseating drop. "What do you mean he went to find me?" she asked with a voice tinged with dread.

AS CAELUM STUDIED HIS SISTER, his eyes tracing over her bruised and weary features, an immense gratitude filled him...Lanae had come back in time to save his ass. The rumblings in the bedroom had been impossible to ignore, and the desperate need to see their parents had overridden every logical reason for not opening that door. He closed his eyes, seeking solace, and pressed his forehead to hers. Her skin was cool, a stark contrast to his own heated flesh.

"Draven went to Xoltan's castle to find you." His whisper was heavy with worry.

She let out a squeak of despair, her breath catching in her throat, and reached inside her shirt.

When she pulled out the green vials, recognition of the portal magic he had seen before registered. He swiped them from her hands with a swift motion, transforming from the devastated younger brother into the protector he had always been. The vials were cold and fragile in his grip, reminding him of the danger they represented.

"You cannot go in your current condition." His voice was firm, yet laced with concern. He climbed to his feet on shaky limbs, every muscle protesting the movement. He nodded toward her wrists, the bindings chafing against her skin. "At least let me get those off, and then we can arm up before we go on another suicide mission."

"I need to get him out of there." Her voice shook as she climbed to her feet, the strain of the situation evident in every syllable.

"And we will, but you need some patching up before we go." His voice was rough, each word scraping his throat now that his own adrenaline had faded. He worked a forceful swallow down his throat and flinched at the pain.

Nero squawked, his voice a piercing cry that echoed in the quiet room. Now that they were both on their feet, the griffin strode up to Lanae, his movements graceful despite his size. He nuzzled her gently, his feathers soft against her skin, before brushing a wing against Caelum. The touch was comforting, almost like a warm embrace, before Nero wrapped Lanae completely in his wings.

Caelum's throat tingled, and he reached up, scraping his fingers over the spot where his father had gripped him. The prickle of pain was fading, the magic of Nero's touch soothing the ache. He swallowed, this time without discomfort. "Thanks, Nero." His voice was filled with gratitude as he ran his hand over the griffin's head.

Nero unfurled from Lanae, tucking his wings neatly against his body before leaving the two of them to stare at each other's unblemished skin. The transformation was almost miraculous, their injuries healed by the griffin's magic.

"I love that griffin." Caelum forced a smile, the expression stretching the muscles of his face in an unfamiliar way after all the stress and pain. He nodded for Lanae to follow him to the kitchen, the promise of a momentary respite giving them both a flicker of hope.

A ROAR OF ANGER had Draven freezing in place. The stone walls, coarse against his back, protected him from being found, but that didn't stop his heart from drumming a staccato beat in his chest.

"She escaped. Find her!"

A wisp of a smile found his lips as he backtracked up the rickety stairs to the last offshoot. He could almost smell her—her familiar lavender scent—as he slid down another secret passage. The damp, musty air clung to his skin, chilling him.

Thundering footsteps shook the walls, causing dust to rain down, and then silence enveloped him.

He shuffled a few feet, the faint lavender scent guiding him like a beacon. The passage narrowed, and he had to hunch over, the stone brushing against his shoulders.

A thud echoed in the hallway, followed by a metallic clang.

"God damned griffin." The angry mutter echoed as if the person was right beyond where Draven stood. He pressed closer to the wall and the vibrations of the voice.

A door creaked open. "Fuck." The curse rippled the surrounding air, sharp and raw. "Are there any left?"

"No, sir. She broke them all."

"I'm going to hunt her down and torture her until her last damned breath." A beat passed. "Start making more."

"But sir..."

A choked sound reverberated through the wall, a strangled gasp.

"You. Start making more of the portal potion."

"Yes, sir." The door slammed shut with a resounding thud.

Draven stayed still and held his breath until the footsteps faded into obscurity. *Portal potion.* He nearly laughed, the sound muffled by the stone surrounding him. His wife had destroyed their ability to move freely from realm to realm. A grin stretched his lips. Her lavender perfume still wafted in the air.

Draven searched for a larger area in the secret passageway that would give him the space to conjure a portal. The narrow, damp corridor was lined with jagged stones that scraped his arms as he moved. He turned a corner and halted, his eyes widening. The dead end before him was the perfect space, a small alcove with just enough room.

He tilted his head to listen. The only sound was the faint brush of footsteps echoing in the distance. The musty scent of mildew clung to the air.

As quietly as possible, he uttered the draconian spell, his voice a hushed whisper that reverberated off the walls. A smile spread across his lips as the gateway opened, shimmering with a soft, iridescent light that revealed the comforting sight of his home. He crossed the threshold, and the portal snapped closed behind him with a soft hiss.

In an instant, a cold, sharp blade pressed against his chest, stopping him in his tracks. The cold, steely scent of the sword mingled with the familiar aroma of lavender.

He lifted his hands at Lanae's narrowed gaze, her eyes filled with suspicion. Her nostrils flared, drawing in a deep breath.

"Lanae, it's me."

"I will not be fooled by your trickery again," she replied, her voice as sharp as the sword she held.

# CHAPTER EIGHT
## *Ally in the Shadows*

*D*ID THE BASTARD REALLY *think she'd fall for this ruse?* She growled, a low, guttural sound, and pushed the tip of her blade through his leathers, smiling when he hissed. The cold steel met resistance, sending a shudder up her arm.

"Um. Lanae?" Caelum stepped into the room, the clinking sound of his lock-pick kit breaking the tension.

"It's the fucking shapeshifter son of that Firetwill asshole," she spat, her voice dripping with venom.

The man's green eyes, so much like Draven's, searched Caelum out in a silent plea for help, a flicker of fear evident in their depths.

"Are you sure that's him?" Caelum's voice held a wariness that made her itch to finish this dick off.

"He liked to screw with my head and use that form when he used his fists." She nodded toward the redheaded giant in their living room, her expression hardening.

"Nero!" Caelum called, his voice firm and commanding.

Lanae swore she saw a fleeting look of relief pass over the shapeshifter's face. It was a far cry from the horror he had displayed when Nero emerged from the bedroom, lightning crackling at his feather tips.

When Nero bolted across the room and nuzzled against Draven, Lanae gasped, her lungs robbed of breath. "You even fooled Nero."

"How did you know the image wasn't me?" Draven's hands remained in the air in surrender, his voice steady.

"I'm not disclosing that to you." Her voice trembled with uncertainty.

His lips tilted into a smile. "There was no electric tingle when we touched. Which was the same way I knew it wasn't you here in our home earlier."

She blinked, his words short-circuiting her brain. Then her gaze dropped to where she pierced his leathers and probably his chest with her sword. If she pushed hard enough, she'd spear his heart. She pulled the blade out, the sound of tearing leather echoing in the room, but she stood her ground. "On your knees."

He dropped slowly to his knees with his palms still facing her, the movement deliberate. He slid one hand behind his head and reached out to her with his other hand. "See for yourself."

"It's a trick." Her insecurity flared, and her heart jumped.

The image of Draven closed his eyes, his breath steady. "Caelum, hold a knife to my throat to make sure I don't move."

Caelum put the lock-pick kit on the table and crossed to Draven, unsheathing the knife on Draven's hip. He held it against the soft flesh of Draven's throat and nodded for Lanae to confirm this was indeed her husband. "If it isn't him, I'll gladly spill his blood."

Fear almost kept Lanae in place, but that small ember of hope ultimately had her moving forward. She lowered the sword and separated her hands as far as the chain would allow before she wiped her free hand against his.

That blessed tingling spark zinged through her, igniting heat in her chest. She dropped the sword.

The metal clattered on the floor. Caelum moved the blade from Draven's neck and stepped away, busying himself with the lock-pick set.

Lanae threw her arms around Draven's head, slamming into his body with the full force of her relief. Her tears dampened his shoulder as she released a sob.

He wrapped his arms around her, pulling her against him so every point on her body was in contact with his. The tender heat from his embrace enveloped her, his heartbeat steady and reassuring against her chest. The tingle of contact chased the fear and doubt from her mind, sending a gentle warmth through her veins. She sagged against him; her legs could no longer support her weight.

"I could have killed you," she whispered, her voice trembling with a mix of relief and guilt.

He kissed her temple; the gentle press of his lips soothed her frayed nerves. "It's only a flesh wound. I'll heal." His breath tickled her skin, carrying a hint of the familiar scent that always calmed her.

She closed her eyes, pressing her cheek against his shoulder. The rough texture of his leather tunic brushed beneath her fingers. The essence of smoke and herbs clung to him, a comforting reminder of home. His arms tightened around her, his hand gently stroking her back in slow, soothing circles.

The room was silent except for their breathing, the tension slowly ebbing away with each shared heartbeat. The rhythm of each steady rise and fall of his chest lulled her into a sense of safety she hadn't felt in days.

"I thought I'd lost you," she said against his skin.

"You'll never lose me," he replied softly, his words a promise that resonated deep within her.

She nodded, her tears soaking into his tunic, but she didn't care. She was home, in his arms, and nothing else mattered.

DRAVEN MET CAELUM'S GAZE. His eyes filled with a silent plea of appreciation, hoping his gratitude would be understood without words. The flickering torchlight cast shadows across

Caelum's face, highlighting the concern in his eyes.

Caelum's cleared throat rasped in the quiet room. "We need to get those cuffs off." He rattled the set in his hands, the clinking of metal echoing sharply.

Lanae sniffled, her breath hitching as she released her hold around Draven's neck. The warmth of her body left him, replaced by a sudden chill.

Draven glanced at the iron cuffs, the cold, unforgiving metal pressing into her wrists. A burn ring, raw and angry, marred her skin underneath, the sight igniting a protective anger within him.

He grabbed her hands, the rough pads of his fingers brushing against her cold, clammy skin as smoke rolled from his nostrils. The bitter fumes of burning filled the air. "What exactly did that bastard do to you?" he growled, his voice rumbling like distant thunder. Iron didn't affect dragons the way it burned the fae. To him, it was only cold metal.

With a furrowed brow and narrowed eyes, he slid his index finger between her wrist and the iron shackle, the metal biting into her flesh. Focusing his fire to a point on the tip of his pad, the heat intensified. The iron glowed a vivid red just before his finger burst through. He sliced through the metal in seconds and tore it away from her tender skin. The stench of scorched iron lingered in the air.

He repeated the process with the second cuff, his actions swift and precise, then crossed to the kitchen. The iron cuffs clattered into a bucket of soapy water with a sharp hiss, steam rising as the water boiled on contact, cooling the searing metal.

Lanae followed, her wrists raw and bloody from the damn iron, the scent of copper mingling with the lingering smoke.

Draven took a drag of a breath, his aura shimmering with residual heat, then turned to meet her gaze. His eyes, a stormy green, softened as they locked onto hers. "You never answered," he murmured, concern threading through his voice.

"You distracted me with your fire." Her lips tilted into a wry smile, her voice a soft whisper. "They did nothing beyond what Nero healed. Just bruises and cuts."

"I should have razed that castle while I had the chance." He locked his gaze with hers. "But I needed to see that you were okay before I rendered it and everyone inside to dust."

CAELUM WIPED THE SWEAT and grime from his face, his brow furrowing as he leaned heavily against the doorway. "Maybe you should have," he muttered, his voice thick with regret and exhaustion.

Both Lanae and Draven turned to look at him, their eyes locking onto his disheveled figure. The air in the tense room charged with unspoken fears and unhealed wounds.

"Look, I was just as uncomfortable leaving that castle standing when we left three years ago," Caelum continued, his voice a low, angry growl. "And now that all those people are reanimated and under another Firetwill's rule, I'm not discounting the opportunity to turn it to ashes."

Lanae's eyes flashed with defiance. "Those people are not responsible for their actions." Her hands trembled despite the evenness of her voice.

"Just like Dad?" Caelum's anger flared, his face contorting with pain and bitterness. "If we unleash Draven from our moral binds, Mom and Dad will be free." He pointed toward the bedroom, where the relentless banging on the door echoed through the hall.

"And we will be no better than the tyrant we are trying to stop."

Lanae's quick volley back ruffled his nerves, her sharp words cutting through the haze of his fury.

Caelum's jaw clenched, the muscles twitching in frustration. Iron and sweat clung to the air, circulating with his recent near-death experience at his father's hands. His heart was a drumbeat of conflicted emotions. He looked at Lanae, her resolve unbroken despite the haunted look in her eyes.

Draven looked beyond him toward the dimly lit hallway, the flickering torchlight casting eerie shadows on the brightly painted walls. "Your parents reanimated?" His voice held a mix of disbelief and concern.

"Yes," Caelum replied, his tone laden with bitterness. "And my father tried to kill me. If Lanae hadn't come back when she did, I would be dead." His words dripped with the acrid bite of betrayal, the memory still raw and painful.

Draven crossed to the heavy wooden bedroom door, his footsteps nearly silent under the babel of bangs. He let out a frustrated roar, a primal sound that reverberated through the space and silenced the relentless pounding. The door shook under his fury, the vibrations resonating through the entire house.

Caelum raised an eyebrow, a flicker of disbelief crossing his features. He had only heard that type of roar from Draven once before—when Xoltan had bound them in the castle, demanding that Lanae provide humiliating favors in front of them. The memory sent a tingle down his back, the echoes of their captor's cruel laughter still fresh in his mind.

When the dragon turned back, his eyes, glowing like molten gold, swept over Caelum, visually inspecting him for any signs of injury. A burning wood scent hovered in the stillness, a signal of his brother-in-law's fiery temper.

Caelum's shoulders tensed under the scrutiny. His recent ordeal played havoc in the weary burn of his muscles. "Nero healed me, too."

"Good," Draven grunted, his voice a low, rumbling growl. But the aggravation remained carved in his features, like cracks in a stone facade.

LANAE WAS JUST AS mystified by Draven's outburst as her brother, her thoughts swirling with confusion and unease. But Nero's approach sidetracked her from them. The griffin closed the distance with a graceful glide, his wings rustling softly as they moved through the air. He gently brushed her wrists with his soft, downy wings, the feathers cool against her skin. The iron burns faded, albeit slower than her bruises and cuts. The tingle of healing took hold, a maddening itch spreading across her skin, and she had to fist her hands to keep from scratching.

"I need some air," Caelum said and left her alone with Draven and her now silent parents.

Draven sauntered back into the living room, his movements heavy with exhaustion. He unclasped his leather armor, the worn straps creaking as they were released, revealing a growing bloody spot on his shirt where her sword had pierced. The faint whiff of blood reached Lanae, tightening her muscles with alarm. She rushed to his side, her heart spasming in a frenzy in her chest. When she reached for his shirt, his hand shot out and grabbed hers, his grip firm but gentle.

"I am all right." His dragon eyes met hers. They gleamed with an inner fire before he blinked, the transformation complete, and his eyes shifted back to the emerald irises that made her knees weak.

"You are bleeding. At least let me clean the wound I caused." Her voice dripped with concern.

"Fine." He stripped his shirt, revealing a deep gouge seeping blood. His muscle-bound chest and tight abs would have made her smile had it not been for the severity of the injury. The coppery scent of blood filled the air, sharp and metallic.

"Fucking hell," she muttered and turned to Nero. "Please fix that cut." She pointed at Draven.

Nero strolled over to Draven, his feathers rustling softly as he moved. He brushed his wing over Draven's chest, the cool touch of his feathers smearing blood on his pristine wings. The griffin's magical healing touch worked, but the process was slow and agonizing.

Draven shifted in the seat, his muscles tensing and his face contorting in pain. He grit his teeth, the pressure building in his jaw. "I swear the itch is sometimes worse than the injury," he growled, his voice strained.

Lanae snorted a laugh, the sound tinged with relief, and left him to deal with the stitching of skin. She grabbed a few wet rags to clean off the blood, the cool water soothing her own raw nerves.

As she returned to Draven's side, she couldn't help but question the outburst. "Draven, what was all that at my parents' door about? It's not like you."

Draven's eyes flickered with unease as memories clawed at his mind. "My worst nightmares, Lanae. Every night, I see what could have happened and when you went missing, I thought the worst."

He took a cleansing breath, the sound shaky and uneven. "I dreamed of you being tortured, hurt, used, and broken. The thought of those nightmares becoming reality..." His voice broke, the vulnerability seeping through his tough exterior.

Lanae's heart clenched at his words, understanding the depth of his fear. The raw emotion in his voice pulled at her soul, and she reached out, her hand gently resting on his arm. The soothing warmth of his skin grounded her from her icy turmoil. "I'm safe now, Draven. They didn't break me."

Draven's eyes softened, the fierce determination in them burning bright. "I told you once that I would burn the universe down for you. I meant it," he whispered, his voice rough with sincerity.

She leaned forward, her breath mingling with his as she pressed her lips to his. The world around them faded away, leaving only the warmth of their embrace. Draven's hand slid into her hair, his fingers tangling in the soft strands as he held her in place. The kiss deepened, a surge of emotions passing between them—love, relief, and a promise of passionate protection.

CAELUM STALKED TOWARD THE barracks, all the frustration and aggression building up in his bones like a coiled snake ready to strike. His breaths were shallow and rapid, the uptick of his heart pounding a relentless rhythm against his ribs. He needed a release, and he knew just where to get it. The echoes of his boots on the cobblestones reverberated through the alleys, each step a resounding declaration of his simmering anger. The damp evening air clung to his skin, mingling with the aroma of rain and earth, grounding him in the present moment.

Granger stepped out of an entrance to a side street, his face shadowed by the dim, flickering rune lights above. The soft hum of the runes mingled with the distant murmur of the barracks, creating an eerie, almost otherworldly ambiance. Granger's presence was a sharp distinction from Caelum's stormy demeanor—an island of calm amidst the turmoil. The cool night breeze ruffled his hair as he took a tentative step forward. His eyes locked onto Caelum's, containing a fusion of respect and apprehension. A light aroma of leather and steel from Granger's armor permeated the air between them.

"Caelum." Granger's voice was steady; a quiet strength behind his words cut through the tension like a blade through fog. "I was hoping you'd come to the barracks. I want to thank you for coming to my aid today. If you hadn't shown up, I'd likely be in the dungeon awaiting a morbid sentence. They take desertion seriously." He cleared his windpipe, the sound echoing softly in the narrow alley. "I owe you a debt of gratitude."

Caelum paused, the strain in his muscles momentarily easing as he regarded Granger. "You don't owe me anything, Granger," he replied, though the roughness in his tone was softened by an undercurrent of sincerity. The flickering light cast fleeting shadows across his face, highlighting the tired lines etched into his skin.

Granger shook his head, taking another step closer, the gravel crunching softly beneath his boots. "No, I do. You saved my position, my life, and that of my family. I do not take things like this for granted." He straightened his posture, the determined resolve reflected in his eyes catching the light. "From this moment on, I swear my loyalty to you. Whatever you need, whenever you need it—you have my word."

A brief silence enveloped them. Granger's oath hung between them like an unspoken promise. The distant sounds of soldiers preparing for the night shift drifted to their ears, reminding them that there was a world beyond their conversation.

Caelum could see the earnestness in Granger's gaze, the unwavering commitment behind his words. Plus, having an elite guard on his side could be a good thing, especially with his entire soldier career shadowed by his sister's accolades.

"Your loyalty is appreciated, Granger," Caelum finally said, a hint of a smile breaking through the hardness of his expression. "And I will hold you to it."

Granger nodded, the sincerity of his vow sealing their bond. As they stood there in the dimly lit alley, a newfound alliance was forged—one that would shape their future friendship in ways neither of them could yet foresee.

# CHAPTER NINE
## *Love and Loyalty*

DRAVEN LEANED HIS FOREHEAD against Lanae's. Her breath mingled with his in the quiet of their living room. The atmosphere was heavy with the lingering scent of lavender and the faint metallic tang of blood. She gently cleaned his chest with a cloth dipped in warm, soapy water, the soft fabric pressing against his skin in soothing strokes. With the banging from outside silenced and Caelum off doing God knew what to relieve his stress, Draven veiled his gaze and savored the sensation of the warm cloth gliding over his chest. He would have continued kissing her, relishing the taste of her lips, but she insisted on cleaning the mess up before they revisited the heat building between them.

"How did your meeting with Varkir go?" Her soft murmur vibrated against his chest.

Her question pulled a weary sigh from his lungs. "Varkir said the Dragon's Heart no longer has any magic or power. But Alestain still wears it on his breastplate." He leaned back and met her gaze, the gravity of his words pulling his lips into a frown.

She nodded, the movement causing her hair to brush lightly against his cheek. "Makes sense," she replied, her tone carrying a note of resigned understanding.

"What do you mean?" He cocked his head, studying her unwavering gaze, the flicker of candlelight casting shadows that danced across her features.

"I saw it. But it wasn't the same as what I saw in your memory. It's just a clear crystal that he has sewn into his leathers over his chest," she explained, her eyes reflecting the dim light.

Draven dropped his head onto the back of the chair, the soft fabric pressing against his scalp as he stared up at the ceiling. "If it had any power left, I would have known while I was in Firetwill's castle." His voice reverberated with frustration and exhaustion.

She put aside the bowl and cloth, the clink of porcelain against wood echoing in the stillness. Climbing into his lap, she wrapped her arms around him, her embrace warm and comforting, banishing the chill that had settled in his bones.

He let out a small, quiet laugh, the sound a rough, dry chuckle that mingled with the crackling of the fireplace. "Varkir also said there was an ancient document somewhere that has the history of the Dragon's Heart, but his network was still looking for it." His voice rumbled low, like distant thunder, as he relayed the information.

She perked up, her eyes widening with a spark of hope. "Oh. That sounds like good news." Her voice was soft, almost musical, cutting through the heavy silence of the room.

"Eh. He wasn't convinced that it would have much insight." He lifted a shoulder in a halfhearted shrug, the movement causing a ripple of pain to spread across his chest. "Either way, I don't know that I'll ever shift again, never mind fly."

"You've had just as bad a day as I've had." She nestled into his shoulder; her hair brushed against his cheek, her scent making him think of a bouquet of roses and wildflowers.

"Yeah, well, I also made the mistake of asking the council and generals in the war room where my wife was." His words were laced with bitterness, the memory of their reactions still fresh in his mind.

Her form stiffened in his arms, and she shot a glare at him, her eyes narrowing with the bite of disbelief. "You what?"

Draven swallowed hard, the column of his throat rippling into a lump, making it difficult to speak. "I was not thinking. Plus, I was frantic to find you, and it was hard enough to get past the guards. I wasn't in the mood to be dicked around by the council." His voice was rough, like sandpaper, as he tried to convey his frustration.

"What happened afterward?" Her pouty lips formed a perfectly kissable scowl as she stared him down with narrowed eyes.

"You came out of the bathroom," he replied, the memory vividly clear in his mind; her eyebrows shot up and her eyes widened in surprise. "And Faide told you to go home. He'd deal with you later."

She blinked wildly, her lashes fluttering like the wings of a butterfly, and then hung her head. "Alestain's son is a shapeshifter."

"I figured someone was, because it certainly wasn't you. Nero wanted nothing to do with you, and your reaction to him being in the house was comical." He chuckled softly, the sound mingling with the crackling of the fireplace.

"How did you know for sure?" Her voice was just a whisper, as if she feared the truth.

He brought his hand up to her cheek, the warmth of her skin against his palm soothing him. "I touched her arm and there was no buzzing electricity between us. And with you, there always is. My nerves hum when we touch." He grinned at her, his eyes crinkling at the corners.

She nodded again, her expression softening like a wilting flower in the evening light. "He nearly fooled me as well." She turned and kissed his palm, her lips warm and soft against his roughened skin, like velvet brushing against stone. The magnetic pull of her gaze never left him.

His smile faltered, the corners of his mouth tugging downward as dark thoughts of what the shapeshifter could have done to his wife clouded his mind. "And?" His unease bloomed, and he tried to anchor himself to her words and not drift into a sea of dreadful possibilities.

"And nothing. But your image freaked Alestain out." She chewed on her lower lip for a moment, her teeth grazing the tender flesh. "Who is Viserion?"

The name of his father, spoken after so many years, brought a bloom of warmth in his chest, like a hearth fire suddenly roaring to life. "My father."

"Your father was the king?"

Her question, filled with innocent curiosity, amused him, as did her wide, imploring eyes, shimmering like moonlit ponds. "Yes. What did you think I meant when I said I was dragon royalty?"

"Royalty covers an awful lot of people." Her eyebrows slowly rose, drawing her forehead into gentle furrows. "That means you are a king."

He shook his head, a soft chuckle escaping his lips. "King of what? There is no monarchy left here. Besides, the council is doing a decent job of running things."

"King of the dragons," she said, as if that meant anything significant.

"Sweetheart, I am the only dragon left." His gaze dropped to her belly. A pang of tenderness and hope flickered in his soul. "Unless you aren't telling me something."

She blanched, the color draining from her face like ink from a washed parchment.

He pulled back, his brows knitting together as he studied her with concern. "You don't want children?"

"I do. Just not now." Her voice was a whisper, heavy with unspoken fears and desires.

His chest tightened, a vise grip of worry squeezing his heart, and he cocked his head, trying to decode her words.

"Not until this business with the Firetwills is over. Besides, you'd be an overprotective ass if I was pregnant during wartime."

Her clarified statement loosened the noose around his chest, a rush of relief flooding him, and he let a smile surface, a light breaking through the storm clouds. "I get it." He would be overbearing and unbearable if she were pregnant, and he knew it. Despite how adept she was with a sword, he would have a great deal of issues with her going out to fight for Solstice City.

The idea of her charging into battle with a baby bump under her armor tickled him in a grim sort of way. He could almost see it—her fierce determination undeterred, belly leading the charge. "Imagine that: you, sword in hand, shield on one arm, and a little warrior in the making on the other." He chuckled softly. "I'd be an anxious wreck."

She arched an eyebrow, a smirk playing at the corners of her lips. "You'd be more than an anxious wreck—you'd be a hawk hovering over the battlefield, and I don't think even the Firetwills would stand a chance against your overprotectiveness."

He barked a laugh, loud and hearty, the sound reverberating through the room and easing the burden from his heart. With a swift, confident motion, he pulled her to his mouth and kissed her deeply, his lips pressing firmly against hers. His arm slid under her knees, cradling her effortlessly as he picked her up without breaking the passionate kiss.

He craved some alone time with her, yearning for the intimacy of their connection. The thought of Caelum walking in on such an intensely private moment sent a wave of unease down his spine. He needed the assurance of their solitude, a sanctuary where he could spoil her undisturbed until she cried out his name.

Draven paced down the hallway to their bedroom, each step echoing in the quiet corridor. His heart danced with anticipation. As he reached the bedroom, he turned the brass knob and entered, closing the door firmly behind him and locking it with a decisive click.

The room enveloped them in a cocoon of warmth and familiarity. A hint of lavender drifted in the air, mixing with the subtle fragrance of her perfume. He gently set her down on the plush bed, the soft fabric yielding to their weight.

His eyes locked onto hers, the intense passion burning between them as strong as the hum of their connection. He reached out, gently brushing a strand of hair away from her face. "It's just us for the next couple of hours," he murmured, his voice low and filled with longing. "No interruptions."

She smiled, a slow, knowing smile that sent a thrill through him. This was their moment, a stolen piece of time just for them.

LANAE CAUGHT THE HEATED spark in his eyes and grinned. It had been a while since they had the time to explore each other. After the hellish time of being captive, she longed for the warmth and comfort of his touch. But she needed to wash away the filth of the dungeon first.

"Can we move this to the bath?" She cocked an eyebrow at him, her voice laced with sultriness, the suggestion hanging in the air like a tantalizing promise.

His smirk widened into an all-out grin, eyes twinkling with anticipation. "I've never had you in the bathtub." His voice hinted at a playful challenge, and he waved for her to lead the way.

A thrill raced down Lanae's spine as she turned and headed toward the bathroom, the cool tiles underfoot contrasting with the warmth radiating from her skin. The soft glow of candlelight flickered in the corners of the room. The scent of lavender and eucalyptus filled the air, a calming yet invigorating blend that seemed to heighten her senses.

She reached the clawfoot tub, its porcelain surface gleaming under the warm light. She started the bath and added her favorite soap powder. The rush of water filled the room like a soothing symphony. The sweet citrus steam curled in the air and created a cocoon of warmth around them.

He approached her from behind, his presence a comforting, solid force. His hands rested on her shoulders, the touch sending a quiver of anticipation through her. He gently turned her to face him, his gaze locking onto hers, embodying a mix of desire and tenderness.

"Let me take care of you," he murmured, his voice a low, velvety promise.

His fingers trail down her arms, igniting a path of sensation. As the tub filled, he helped her in, the warm water enveloping her like a comforting embrace. He followed, settling in behind her, his chest pressed against her back, his arms wrapping around her in a protective hold.

The water lapped gently around them, and they sank into the tranquility of the moment, their connection deepening in the quiet refuge of the bath. His hands roamed her body, not in urgency but in reverence, as if rediscovering every curve and line.

"I love you, Lanae Emberwing."

His soft whisper sent a wave of gooseflesh over her arms, and her nipples hardened under the soft, kneading stroke of his fingers. When his lips brushed her neck, she tilted her head back to give his mouth more access. The tickle of his tongue glided from the base of her throat to her ear, creating a molten heat in her core.

She moaned softly as his fingers danced over the bud at the apex of her thighs, heightening every nerve in her body. He played her like a fine instrument until a tidal wave of passion crashed through her. Her pants echoed on the marble walls, and he covered her mouth with his, tangling his tongue with hers in a sensuous war for dominance.

Lanae twisted in his grip and straddled his lap, lowering herself onto his hard member in slow sweetness. Her head tilted back in ecstasy as she slowly rode him. The water sloshed around them, cresting and ebbing in the same rhythm as their bodies.

She pressed her mouth to his, swallowing their keening desire. The kiss transcended time and space, launching them into a blissful orbit as they surfed the wave of passion beyond the flash point.

CAELUM STORMED DIRECTLY TO the sparring room, his jaw clenched and his heartbeat thundering in his ears. He needed to punch, hit, or swing a wooden sword until the searing hurt ripping through his muscles drowned out the anguish gnawing at his core. The last hour at home had been an unrelenting nightmare. The memory of his parents' blank stares, void of recognition, twisted like a knife in his chest. It wasn't until Lanae entered that any semblance of familiarity flickered in their eyes. And it was all because of her.

Jealousy was a venomous thing, he knew, but he couldn't help the bitterness that rose in his throat whenever the relentless comparisons to his sister shadowed him like an oppressive fog.

He stepped into the training hall, the warm glow of candlelight flickering against the stone walls. He stalled at the door, his breath catching in his throat. Only one soldier was inside, and her presence stole the air from his lungs. Jenna moved with a fluid grace, her maneuvers a dance of precision and power that left him in silent awe.

Caelum watched Jenna's every move, his own body tense and still as her elegance mesmerized him. The rhythmic sounds of her practiced motions filled the hall, echoing softly against the ancient stone. Her intensity and focus radiated from her, the way her muscles coiled and released with every swing of her sword.

He took a rapid pull of wind into his lungs, the cool air of the training hall mingling with the warmth of the candlelight, creating a strange, calming contrast. For a moment, the troubles of the past hour seemed to lift, replaced by the serenity of Jenna's fluidity and strength.

Finally, Jenna paused, as if sensing his presence. She turned, her eyes locking onto his, and a small, knowing smile curved her lips. "Caelum," she greeted, her voice smooth and steady. "You look like you could use some sparring."

He managed a nod, his voice caught in his throat. "I... I need to clear my head."

Jenna's expression softened, understanding flickering in her gaze. "Then let's begin." She handed him a wooden sword. "Sometimes, the best way to silence the chaos inside is through movement."

As they squared off, the tension in Caelum's body dissolved. With each clash of their swords, his frustration and jealousy channeled into something productive, something he could control. The physical exertion was a welcome distraction from the emotional turmoil, and for the first time in hours, a semblance of peace settled in his soul.

Through the sparring, Jenna's encouragement and guidance were like a balm to his troubled soul. Her presence, her strength, and her quiet understanding made all the difference, helping him find his balance amidst the storm.

As they finished the final round, both breathing heavily, Jenna lowered her sword and stepped closer. Caelum's heart swelled, a different tension rising within him. He hesitated for a moment, searching her eyes for any sign of uncertainty, but found only warmth and an unspoken understanding.

With a tentative step forward, he closed the distance between them. Jenna tilted her head, her gaze unwavering. Tentatively, Caelum leaned in, capturing her lips in a soft, tender kiss. The world melted away, giving him a brief respite from the chaos and pain that had consumed him.

A throat cleared, shattering the delicate intimacy of the moment, and Caelum stepped away from Jenna as if she were on fire. His skin prickled with sudden, icy awareness.

"You know that's not allowed." Granger's fierce scowl and crossed arms filled the doorway to the training room, his voice a growl of reprimand. The flickering candlelight cast harsh shadows on his stern features, emphasizing the disapproval etched into every line of his face.

Caelum's heart froze mid-beat and then launched into a tirade, anger and frustration bubbling to the surface. "I didn't think I'd be calling in that favor so soon," he snapped back, his voice tight with barely restrained fury. The air cracked with unresolved tension, their unsaid words pressing down like a heavy storm cloud.

Granger's eyes narrowed, a spark of recognition flickering in their depths. "You're playing a dangerous game, Caelum," he warned, his tone icy. "One misstep, and you'll lose more than just your privileges here."

Caelum's jaw clenched, the bitterness of the last hour resurfacing with a vengeance. "I've already lost my parents, Granger," he retorted, his voice raw. "What's a little more risk compared to that?"

Granger's gaze softened, a rare glimpse of empathy breaking through his hardened exterior. He sighed, the tightness in his shoulders easing. "Just be careful," he muttered, stepping aside to let Caelum and Jenna pass. "Don't let your emotions cloud your judgment."

Caelum nodded curtly, his mind a whirlwind of conflicting thoughts. He glanced at Jenna, her eyes filled with unspoken concern and support. Despite the prevailing chaos, her presence grounded him, providing a fleeting sense of stability.

As they left the training hall, Caelum couldn't shake the impression that this was just the beginning of something predestined. With Jenna by his side, a glimmer of hope sparked his determination into a flame that refused to be extinguished.

# CHAPTER TEN
## *A Plea for Mercy*

MORNING CAME FASTER THAN either of them wanted, and Lanae groaned as she rolled into her pillow, its linen surface cool against her cheek. Draven grumbled, his deep voice vibrating through his chest as he pulled her tighter, cocooning her in his warmth. She sighed, savoring the moment, the mingling scents of pine and leather from his skin enveloping her.

"I need to get up and get ready to go to the training grounds." Her voice was a murmur, reluctant to break the spell of their shared stillness. She rubbed his arms, kneading the taut muscles beneath her fingers, before peeling them off her and climbing out of bed. The cold air hit her skin like a wake-up call, and she shivered, glancing back at Draven, who now lay sprawled across the bed, his auburn hair fanning out on the pillow.

A sharp knock on the door interrupted her thoughts, echoing through the quiet room. She pulled on her robe, the soft, worn fabric brushing against her skin, and hurried to the door. The cold stone floor sent a chill up her spine with each step. As she opened the door, the scent of his honey tea wafted in, circulating with the faint aroma of candles burning low.

Caelum stood outside her bedroom, his posture rigid, a sealed scroll bearing the Council crest clutched in his hand. His eyes were shadowed with fatigue, matching the lines of exhaustion etched on his face. The golden crest shimmered, highlighting the dark circles under his eyes. He looked just as exhausted as she was. A silent understanding passed between them as she reached for the scroll, its weight heavier than the parchment itself.

Lanae took the missive, breaking the seal with trembling fingers. The parchment crinkled as she unrolled it, her eyes scanning the formal script.

*Captain Nightshade,*

*You are hereby summoned to appear before the Council immediately to discuss matters of grave importance. Your presence is not only requested, but demanded.*

*By the authority of the Fae Council*

Lanae's heart thundered as she read the words, each line of the summons etching an icy dread into her chest. She met Caelum's gaze, his tired eyes reflecting her own unease; the Council's demands draped on her shoulders like an invisible burden. The echo of Draven's confession from yesterday still lingered in her mind, sharp and troubling.

"I guess I should head to the training yard without you?" Caelum cocked an eyebrow, his voice a tentative bridge between their shared worries.

Lanae nodded, the motion causing a strand of her hair to fall across her face. She brushed it away absently, her mind already racing with the implications of Draven's slip-up. The scent of burning wood from the fireplace mingled with the crisp morning air, grounding her in the present moment.

She looked back at Draven, who had propped himself up on one elbow, his expression now serious. The playfulness of their earlier moments had vanished, replaced by a steely resolve in his eyes. His hair, tousled and dark, framed his face, shadowing his determined gaze. The atmosphere grew colder, the profound implications settling over them like a winter frost.

"It seems I have more pressing matters than training today." She handed Draven the scroll.

He scanned the parchment, the furrow in his brow deepening with each line. His grip on the scroll tightened, the paper crinkling under the pressure. "We better get ready," Draven replied. The determination in his tone was mirrored by the way he swung his legs over the side of the bed, the mattress creaking softly in protest.

"This is for me to appear, not us," she started, her voice catching as the enormity of the situation hit her anew. The scent of parchment and ink seemed to cling to her fingers, a tangible reinforcement of the Council's authority.

"Look, I got you into this mess. I'm not letting you take the fall alone. Besides, their rationale for not approving our marriage was ludicrous." Draven's words were filled with conviction. He reached his hand out, clasping hers. The strength in his grip relayed his unspoken promise to stand by her, no matter the cost.

The day that had begun with warmth and comfort now loomed with the uncertainty of what lay ahead. The soft light of dawn filtered through the curtains, casting a golden hue over their faces, magnifying the growing tension in the room. The air seemed heavier, laden with the grim anticipation of the Council's demands. The faint aroma of morning dew mingled with the lingering scent of the night's embers, grounding them in the present moment. They shared a fleeting glance, a silent acknowledgment of the challenges they were about to face together.

"Besides, I am the king of the dragons." He flashed her a cheeky smile, his eyes twinkling with mischief. The corners of his mouth curled upward, breaking through the tension like a ray of sunshine piercing through storm clouds.

DRAVEN SLIPPED INTO THE kitchen while Lanae finished dressing, the faint clinking of utensils and soft sizzle of the stove filling the quiet morning air. The aroma of freshly cracked eggs mingled with the scent of buttered toast, creating a comforting symphony of breakfast fragrances. He whisked the eggs with practiced ease, the golden yolks swirling into a creamy mixture, before pouring them into the hot pan. The toast popped up, perfectly browned, and he spread a thin layer of butter, watching it melt and seep into the warm bread.

Nero squawked, his feathers ruffling in agitation as he tried to steal a piece of toast from the tray. The crisp, buttery aroma of the toast seemed to tempt the griffin beyond reason. Draven growled a warning, his voice a low rumble that made Nero pause. The griffin's sharp beak hovered inches from the toast before he reluctantly backed off, his golden eyes glinting with frustration.

While the eggs cooked, filling the kitchen with the savory scent of breakfast, Draven opened the back door. The cool morning air rushed in, carrying the earthy fragrance of damp soil and fresh grass. He gestured for Nero to step outside. "Go get your own food. But remember the rules."

Nero gave one last disgruntled squawk before hopping out, his wings unfurling as he prepared to take flight. The clatter of his talons clicking against the stone patio faded as he disappeared into the early light.

Draven quickly returned to the stove, the faint hiss and sizzle of the eggs reminding him to act swiftly. He retrieved the eggs just before they browned too much, their savory aroma filling the kitchen. Carefully, he set the plate of eggs and toast on a tray, the golden hue of the toast complementing the fluffy eggs. Beside them, glasses of freshly squeezed orange juice gleamed in the morning light, their citrusy tang adding a refreshing note to the meal. The tray, with its carefully arranged components, was a picture of simplicity and care, a small island of normalcy amidst the morning's tension.

Lanae came in a few minutes later, her footsteps soft against the kitchen floor. She stared at the tray, her eyebrows knitting together in confusion. "We don't have time to eat," she said with a tongue that could shear a sheep.

"I know. But your parents are awake and will need nourishment," Draven replied, his tone gentle yet firm. He reached out, handing her a glass of juice, the cool condensation dampening his fingers.

She blinked at him as if the thought hadn't even crossed her mind, the realization dawning slowly. The room was filled with the mingling scents of breakfast and the unspoken weight of their responsibilities, a quiet testament to the care and consideration Draven had taken amidst their chaos.

"I don't think Caelum thought to feed them either." She drank what Draven offered and then placed the empty glass in the soapy water in the sink, the bubbles clinging to the rim as it sank into the foam.

Draven headed down the dimly lit hallway to her parents' bedroom with Lanae following him. The scrape of their footsteps echoed softly against the stone walls, the faint creaking of floorboards under their feet added a rhythm to their steps.

Balancing the tray carefully, Draven reached up to the top of the door molding, his fingers brushing against the smooth wood before finding the hidden key. The cool metal was reassuring in his grasp as he brought it down, the quiet clink of the key sounding like a small but significant moment amidst the morning's unfolding events.

He swung the door open, the hinges creaking softly in the early morning quiet. The room was dimly lit, the heavy drapes drawn tight, allowing only slivers of dawn light to filter through. The air inside was thick with a musty scent, mixing with the faint aroma of the breakfast tray.

As they stepped inside, Lanae's parents, disheveled and wild-eyed, lunged toward them. Her mother's once gentle hands now clawed at the air, and her father's eyes, usually filled with wisdom, were clouded with a frantic desperation.

Draven reacted quickly, balancing the tray with one hand while raising his free arm to fend off her parents' frantic attacks. The eggs wobbled precariously on the plate, and the juice threatened to spill over the rim of the glasses.

Lanae stepped forward, her voice steady yet urgent. "Mother, Father. Please, calm down. We brought you food." Her words seemed to pierce through the haze of their minds, and for a moment, there was a flicker in their eyes.

Her father hesitated, his movements slowing as he stared at her and then at the tray Draven had balanced on his hand. Her mother's hands dropped as if she understood her body's needs, her breathing ragged as she took a step back.

Draven carefully set the tray down on a nearby table, the clinking of the glasses a small sound amidst the tension. The aroma of the warm breakfast filled the room.

Lanae moved closer to her parents, her hands raised in a gesture of peace. "We brought you breakfast. Please, sit down and eat. You need your strength." The soothing scent of the eggs and toast seemed to reach them, and slowly, they calmed, their frantic energy dissipating.

Draven's muscles tensed, his senses sharp and ready to react if needed. The room was charged with the anticipation of potential conflict, the air heavy with the scent of breakfast and lingering tension. But as the moments passed, the familiar, comforting scent of eggs and toast, along with the grumbling of Lanae's parents' stomachs, coaxed them to the table without further incident. Their hunger overpowered their agitation, and they ate in silence, the clinking of cutlery a gentle, reassuring sound in the background.

Lanae backed out of the room, the flutter of her heart visible in the throbbing vein in her neck. The cool air in the hallway contrasted with the tension-laden warmth of the room.

Draven followed closely behind, the creak of floorboards under his boots the only sound breaking the silence, unwilling to turn his back on her parents even for a second. He locked the door with a soft click; the sound echoed in the quiet. He measured the metal key's weight, a small anchor of normalcy, before he let it go and returned it to its hiding place atop the door molding.

Then he wrapped Lanae in a hug, his arms encircling her with warmth and strength. The sensation of her pressing against his solid chest offered a small measure of comfort, a buffer against the turmoil that was evident in her eyes. The tension slowly eased from her body, and he held her close, his own resolve bolstered by the simple act of being there for her.

"We need to go," he said, even though he just wanted to stay here and hold her until the sadness in her eyes disappeared. The slight tremor in her shoulders as she inhaled through her nostrils resonated deep within him.

When she pulled away, the walls closed in on them as their reckoning loomed ahead.

LANAE THREADED HER FINGERS through Draven's as they drew near the Citadel. The cool, smooth touch of his skin against hers was a small anchor in the whirlwind of her emotions. Her nerves left her jumpy, each rustle of leaves and distant murmur of the city making her heart race. But the steady hum of their connection calmed her and gave her the steel spine she would need in front of the council.

She led Draven through the grand atrium, the soft echo of their footsteps resonating in the vast space. As they ventured deeper into the belly of the building, the air grew thick with the rich aroma of ancient wood and lingering traces of magic. The enormous tree at the center of the Citadel sprouted from the ground, its majestic branches growing beyond the top of the tower, casting dappled light that danced on the stone floor.

The winding staircase, intricately carved into the tree's bark, spiraled upward, inviting them to ascend. The texture of the bark was rough under her fingers as she gripped the railing for balance. Lanae led the charge up the stairs, the ascent making her dizzy as they climbed higher and higher. Halfway up, they reached an arched doorway leading to the council court, seamlessly carved within the great tree.

The council seats were masterpieces, their intricate designs showcasing the skill of the artisans who crafted them. The wood surrounding the floor was a rich tapestry of swirling patterns and delicate carvings, where guests and dignitaries once voiced their grievances. Today, it was where Lanae and Draven would submit to the council's questions.

The guest seats were carved to match the council member seats, each one resembling woven tree limbs, down to the finely detailed leaves. But they were empty today. Only the council graced this hall, and all eyes were on Lanae and Draven as they stepped into the center. The council's scrutiny was heavy on their shoulders while they waited for the flurry of accusations to fall.

Faide Frostvale stood before them, his usually stoic features marred with barely concealed anger. His violet eyes blazed with such force that Lanae's skin prickled. The room thickened with tension as Faide pointed an accusatory finger at Draven.

"Why is he here?" Faide's voice was sharp, each word like a dagger thrown into the stillness.

Draven's chest puffed out in defiance, ready to speak, but Lanae quickly squeezed his hand, catching his attention. The fiery energy of his palm against hers was a fleeting comfort amidst the rising storm.

"Because he is my husband and whatever punishment you seek to enact, he stands with me." Her voice was firm, each word a shield against the council's impending judgment.

Smoke billowed from Draven's nose, a visible sign of his mounting anger. He released Lanae's hand, crossing his arms over his chest. The muscles in his jaw jumped with restrained fury. "You know who I am, right?" His voice carried the edge of violence, a low growl that reverberated through the room.

Faide stared at him, his gaze unyielding. "You are a dragon."

Draven inclined his head, acknowledging the truth. Lanae opened her mouth to speak, but Draven put his hand out to stop her, his gesture commanding silence.

"Lanae is a superb warrior and a passionate woman. The kind of woman who is fit to be a queen."

The bold proclamation sent murmurs rippling through the council. Many of the members leaned forward with wide-eyed stares.

Warning bells clamored in Lanae's head, an uproar of fear and apprehension. "Draven," she whispered, but he cut a glare at her, silencing her with a look.

"I know the council has Solstice City's best interest at heart, which is why I have not laid my claim on this realm. But understand this: if you move to punish her for marrying me, then I will have to rethink my position." His voice was unwavering, the words carrying an unspoken threat.

"And what position is that?" Faide snarled, his anger barely restrained.

"I am the son of Viserion Emberwing."

The declaration sent a shock wave through the council. A few of the older members recoiled, their eyes wide with disbelief.

Draven's gaze pinned them with an unwavering intensity. "And as the son of the dragon king, the throne is rightfully mine."

Lanae held her breath, her heart picking up speed. This was not what she wanted. She had not come here for a showdown that would question the council's validity.

"From the looks on a couple of your faces, it seems you remember my father. But do you recognize who nearly wiped this city off the map?" Draven's voice echoed in the tense silence of the council chamber. The air crackled with Draven's unspoken threat hanging like a storm cloud over their heads.

"Your father," one of the bolder elderly council members said, their voice wavering but holding a note of defiance.

The chamber seemed to hold its breath, the tension like a live wire cascading across the floor.

Draven's sarcastic and bitter laugh filled the room, echoing off the wooden walls. It was a sound that cut through the air like a knife, filled with years of pent-up frustration and anger. "No." His voice dripped with disdain. "Alestain Firetwill cursed my father with the same type of mind control that you witnessed three years ago in our last skirmish with the Firetwills."

A chill ran through the air.

He continued, his tone laced with bitterness. "And then he stole the Dragon's Heart and used it to rid this realm of dragons and fae enemies alike."

The silence that followed was heavy, filled with the unspoken realization of the severity of Alestain's actions. The flickering torchlight cast eerie shadows across the council members' faces, their expressions ranging from shock to disbelief. The air charged with a storm of emotions that brewed beneath the surface as Draven's revelation sank in.

"You have laid blame on the dragons when it was one of your own who brought this realm to its knees." Draven's accusation flung out like a whip. His voice launched through the air with the force of a physical blow. The room vibrated with the intensity of his words, the echoes lingering in the charged atmosphere.

His eyes burned with a fierce, indignant light, and the muscles in his jaw tightened as he spoke. "We are protectors by nature. Not the war-mongering beasts you made us out to be." The heat of his anger radiated from him, and the council members recoiled, his accusation layering over them like a heavy shroud.

"And now Alestain Firetwill has woken his brother's army and will come to enact his final revenge on this city." Draven's voice resonated through the chamber, each word a harbinger of the impending doom.

The council members exchanged anxious glances, their eyes wide with the news.

He glanced at Lanae, the intensity of his gaze a silent acknowledgment of her bravery. "But not as quickly as we assumed because Lanae destroyed his ability to travel realms before she escaped his prison."

The council members' whispers filled the room like the rustling of leaves in a storm. Some leaned forward in their seats, their brows furrowed in contemplation, while others reclined, their expressions a blend of disbelief and grudging respect.

Faide's mouth popped open, and the anger in his eyes gave way to a flicker of something akin to respect.

The reality of Alestain's threat sunk in. The soft murmurs of the council became a backdrop to the sense of urgency that now pervaded the chamber, each member grappling with the implications of the news. The enormity of what lay ahead was undeniable.

"We are aware that the mind-controlled have woken. The dungeons are active with them trying to escape, as if the call to action has severed their ability to rationalize." Faide's voice echoed through the chamber like a stiff wind. His eyes still blazed with barely contained anger. "And while we were warned of the imposter in our midst yesterday, that still does not lessen Lanae's betrayal. She went behind our backs after we explicitly denied your union."

The tension in the room thickened. The council members shifted uneasily in their seats, their expressions carved with disapproval. The soft rustling of robes and the creak of wooden seats added a sense of foreboding to the moment.

The ridiculousness of Faide's accusation stung like a physical blow. The heavy silence amplified the magnitude of his words and sparked the fight within her. Draven's presence beside her was a reassuring anchor, his steady breath and the radiant comfort of his proximity grounding her amidst the council's misplaced judgment.

"My private life has no bearing on my ability to defend this city." Lanae's voice echoed off the timber walls, reverberating through the chamber like a clarion call. "I love Draven Emberwing and will defend him just as vehemently as I do this city. I did not require your approval to join my heart to his. It was not a betrayal of my position or of my loyalty to you."

Her anger at their judgment flared bright, a fierce heat that seemed to radiate from her very being. The intensity of her emotions caused fresh growth to sprout from the ancient walls, delicate vines unfurling and creeping up the wood, their leaves glistening with a vibrant green.

The council members watched in stunned silence, their eyes wide as they witnessed the tangible manifestation of her power. The cavernous space seemed to come alive with the pulsating rhythm of her determination, the recent growth serving as a testament to her power. The flickering torchlight danced across the fresh foliage, casting intricate shadows that mirrored the complex emotions swirling within the chamber.

Faide waved at the ivy vines crawling up the walls, their leaves rustling softly in the otherwise tense silence. "This is why we did not sanction the union. Your offspring will be the death of this city," he declared, his voice cold and unwavering.

His words hung like a dark cloud overshadowing the room.

"Our offspring are none of your concern." Draven's statement carried a finality that fell like a bomb, the room recoiling from the impact. The air crackled with the dragon's silent threat, leaving everyone in the room on edge.

Lanae drew a lungful of oxygen, calming the mounting anger inside her. The cool air grounded her as she prepared to address the council. "We can have a discussion relating to your fears about our relationship later. Right now, we have a more pressing issue. Alestain wants Solstice City to be a monarchy that *he* leads. He is the threat we need to face. Not Draven."

Her voice was steady and commanding, each word resonating with conviction. The council members exchanged uneasy glances, their faces etched with combining elements of reluctance and recognition of the truth in her words. The air in the room seemed to grow thicker, the scent of the ancient tree mingling with the subtle aroma of tension and uncertainty.

Faide's eyes flickered as anger slowly gave way to contemplation. He glanced around the room, noting the pensive expressions of his fellow council members.

One of the elder council members, a fae with silver hair and a wise, contemplative gaze, leaned forward. "Alestain is the immediate threat we must address. His ambitions endanger the very foundation of our city."

Murmurs of agreement rippled through the council, the impending threat uniting them in a common cause. The room hummed with the collective resolve of the council, the ancient magic that permeated the Citadel responding to their determination.

Faide let out a heavy sigh, the stiffness in his shoulders visibly easing. "Very well," he conceded, his voice softer but still authoritative. "For now, we must focus our efforts on defending Solstice City from Alestain's forces. We will address the matter of your union at a later time."

Draven's grip on Lanae's hand tightened briefly, a silent acknowledgment of the minor victory. The air lightened as the oppressive weight of judgment lifted. The council members nodded in agreement, their expressions shifting from accusation to determination.

"What of your parents?" Faide asked, his voice softened by a hint of empathy, the usual animosity tempered by the seriousness of the situation. His eyes, though still stern, held a flicker of concern.

"They are awake, but they do not recognize Caelum or me." Lanae's voice trembled as she spoke, each word a bitter pill that she forced herself to swallow. The burden of her parents' condition brought forth her sense of helplessness and sorrow. The sting of tears bloomed in the back of her eyes, but she blinked them away, drawing strength from the power within her.

"I don't know what strategies you and the generals have planned, but I must implore you to curtail the killing if we are attacked." Her voice steadied, taking on a pleading tone as she addressed the council. "These people fighting with Alestain are not of sound mind. They do not have a will of their own." The enormity of the statement lingered, the realization of the enemy's plight adding a layer of complexity to their struggle.

"In order to free them from their prison, we have to eliminate the Firetwill line." Her words were a somber proclamation, the finality of the solution settling over the council like a shroud.

The council members exchanged glances, their faces reflecting a range of emotions, from reluctance to grim determination. The air was thick with the unspoken understanding that their actions would shape the future of Solstice City. Faide's gaze softened further, the flicker of concern now a steady flame. The shared burden bound them together in the face of the coming storm.

# CHAPTER ELEVEN
## *The Calm Before the Storm*

CAELUM BLOCKED ANOTHER BLOW from his sparring partner, the clash of wooden swords echoing through the training yard. Sweat trickled down his brow, stinging his eyes as he moved with practiced precision. The musty scent of old leather and iron filled his nostrils, mingling with the slight tang of blood from a scrape on his arm. Each strike reverberated through his bones in a testament to the physical demands of his training.

Yet his mind was miles away, replaying the memory of Jenna's kiss. He could still feel the softness of her lips and the warmth that spread through him, igniting a fire in his chest. The world had seemed to stop in that moment, the noise of the training room fading into a distant hum. Her scent—fresh like a field of wildflowers—lingered in his memory, a constant distraction from his sparring. His thoughts danced around the way her eyes sparkled with mischief, the way her laughter rang like a melody he couldn't quite get out of his head.

A sudden, forceful strike brought him back to the present, the impact jarring his arm painfully. He winced, tightening his grip on the sword. His sparring partner's breathing was heavy, mirroring his own exhaustion. Caelum shook his head, trying to refocus on the fight, but Jenna's presence was a persistent shadow in his thoughts, making each movement both automatic and surreal.

He yielded after another blow, his muscles aching from the relentless sparring. Dropping his sword to the ground, he trudged toward the cooler, his mouth dry and parched. The anticipation of the crisp, cool water made his steps quicker. As he reached the water trough, he grabbed a metal cup, relishing the coolness against his palm. He poured himself a drink; the water cascaded in a sparkling stream that splashed gently onto the rim.

He took a long, refreshing gulp, the icy liquid soothing his dry throat and revitalizing his senses. Wiping his brow with his arm, he sighed in relief, the brief respite giving him a moment to collect his thoughts.

His gaze wandered to the neighboring fields, where the more senior soldiers practiced with a disciplined grace. Their precise movements and the clash of steel echoed through the air, a symphony of martial prowess. Among them, his eyes homed in on the object of his growing desire—Jenna. She moved with fluid elegance, her every motion exuding confidence and skill. The sunlight caught her hair, creating a halo of golden light around her, making her stand out even more vividly against the backdrop of the training ground.

Caelum's chest thrummed wildly as he watched her, the memory of their kiss lingering in his mind. His senses were heightened, every detail of the moment etched into his memory—the softness of her lips, the sweet scent of her skin, the warmth that had enveloped him. He couldn't help but be drawn to her, his thoughts consumed by her presence even as he stood on the sidelines. The desire to be near her, to experience that connection again, was a fire that burned within him, making it hard to focus on anything else.

When Jenna finished sparring, she wiped a bead of sweat from her forehead and scanned the field. Her eyes quickly found him, a warm glow spreading across her face as she caught sight of Caelum.

The hint of a smile that tilted her lips was enough to send a rush of heat through his soul, melting away the exhaustion of the day.

Before he could savor the moment, a loud commotion erupted at the far end of the yard. Caelum's heart skipped a beat as Nero bounded toward the training field. Nero's powerful wings flapped, sending gusts of wind that kicked up clouds of dust. In his sharp talons hung the carcass of a cow, and his fierce golden eyes gleamed with mischief.

The griffin's arrival was a whirlwind of chaos. Caelum hung his head, swearing under his breath as the griffin circled the sparring field, drizzling soldiers with fresh blood. The coppery scent filled the air, blending with the earthy aroma of disturbed soil and the musty scent of sweat. Nero cawed triumphantly, as if his kill represented a badge of honor. The beast knew the rules. Draven was going to roast him alive.

Soldiers scattered in all directions, trying to avoid the troublemaking creature. The sound of armor clanking and hurried footsteps echoed around the field. At least they weren't cowering in fear like the prior day when Nero exercised his storm powers, summoning dark clouds and lightning. The environment was charged with the pungent scent of death, and the occasional breeze carried the whiff of fresh blood.

With an air of dominance, Nero came to a halt just a few paces from Jenna. His feathers shimmered in the sunlight, an array of pastel blues, vibrant pinks, and rich purples that were both beautiful and terrifying. He spread his wings wide, casting an enormous shadow over the training ground, as if challenging anyone who dared come near his meal. The sunlight glinted off his sharp beak, highlighting its lethal curve.

Caelum's hands balled into fists at his sides, his knuckles whitening. He crossed the grounds with determined strides, marching right up to the griffin. His breath quickened with the fury filling him, each exhale a harsh sign of his mounting anger. The closer he got, the more the oppressive heat radiated from the beast.

"What do you think you're doing?" he snapped, his voice a strained growl.

Nero's gaze flicked to Caelum with a glint of mischief. He lowered his head, and with a quick, savage motion, took a chunk of meat out of the dead bovine in his talon, gobbling it down. The sound of tearing flesh was sickeningly audible, making Caelum grit his teeth.

Jenna's hand landed gently on Caelum's arm, urging him away from the beast. Her touch was soft, a vivid disparity to the roughness of the situation.

He covered her hand with his and squeezed, drawing strength from her presence. "Nero won't hurt me," he assured her, his voice steady but tense.

Nero's head tilted, as if mocking Caelum. The griffin's eyes sparkled with a mischievous glint, seeming to understand the trouble he was causing.

Caelum put his hands on his waist and stared at the creature, his thoughts racing. The last time Nero grabbed livestock, they had been warned by the council of the consequences if it were to happen again. The memory of that stern reprimand made his pulse pound in his ears, adrenaline sharp on his tongue. "They will demand reparations, Nero." His low voice was filled with warning.

Nero cawed loudly, a sound that echoed across the field, and then took to the skies with his meal, powerful wings stirring the air into a frenzy. The gusts of wind carried the scent of death and disrupted the peace of the training ground. But the damage had been done, and all the guards would be talking about was the damned griffin and his propensity to pillage their livestock.

Caelum watched him go, a mix of frustration and resignation settling over him.

He turned to Jenna, shaking his head with a wry smile. "I'm sorry. He's in a teen phase." He shrugged, as if that explained everything.

Jenna burst out laughing, the sound a sweet, musical relief against the tension hanging in the air. Her eyes sparkled with amusement, her laughter sending ripples through the stifling atmosphere. "Griffins are dangerous, Caelum," she said between chuckles, wiping away a tear of laughter from the corner of her eye.

Caelum lifted a brow, the corners of his mouth twitching in a playful smirk. "Just like dragons?" His voice was light and teasing.

Her laughter bubbled up again, and the sound was contagious. The way her eyes crinkled and her shoulders shook made it impossible not to join in. Caelum chuckled too, the shared moment of humor breaking the tension and lightening his spirits. It was a pleasant distraction from the chaos of the last few days, a gentle prod that even in the midst of trouble, there could still be moments of levity.

Their laughter echoed across the training ground, drawing curious glances from the other soldiers. Despite the blood-streaked field and the distant figure of Nero in the sky, for a brief moment, everything seemed right in the world.

"I'm heading off to clean up. Care to join me?" Jenna hooked her thumb toward the neatly lined houses where most of the soldiers lived. The houses, though simple, stood in orderly rows, their wooden frames weathered by time but well-kept. A fragrant mix of soap and fresh laundry wafted from the direction of the barracks, promising a reprieve from the grime of the training field.

Caelum glanced around, his eyes flitting between his sparring partner, the bustling training grounds, and the houses. The clinking of swords and the shouts of soldiers practicing filled the air. He knew he should decline, but the way his soul cried out for her was more powerful than getting into trouble with his superiors. A magnetic pull toward her filled him, a warmth that called him away from the rigid structure of his training routine.

After all, what he did on his lunch break really shouldn't be monitored by the powers that be. The thought brought a smirk to his lips, a hint of rebellion sparking in his chest. He could almost hear the distant chatter of his comrades, see the knowing glances they'd exchange if they saw him leave with Jenna. Yet, the prospect of spending even a few moments in her company outweighed the potential reprimand.

He took a step toward her, the decision made. The dusty ground crunched beneath his boots, and the cool breeze caressed his flushed skin, bringing with it the mingled scents of pine and earth. "Lead the way." His steady voice trembled with anticipation. As they walked side by side, the noise of the training ground faded behind them, replaced by the quieter, more intimate sounds of their shared steps and the crunch of leaves in the wind.

Caelum's heart pounded in tune with the carnal thoughts breezing through his mind as he followed her into her small cottage. The door groaned open, and a comforting warmth greeted him. The wooden floorboards creaked underfoot, each step echoing the rhythm of his racing pulse. The soft afternoon sunlight filtered through the windows and danced on the walls, shaping shadows that swayed like ghosts in a silent waltz. The cozy space was adorned with handmade quilts and rustic furniture, evoking a sense of simplicity. As his eyes adjusted to the change from the bright sunshine outdoors, his gaze fell on a small fireplace with the remains of a fire still burning, its warmth spreading through the room like a tender embrace. The crackling embers and the gentle ticking of an old clock on the mantelpiece created a soothing symphony that seemed to calm his racing thoughts.

The gentle creak of the door closing sent his pulse pounding, and he turned to Jenna. A soft ray of sunlight highlighted her face, making her eyes sparkle like twin stars. "Cute place." He forced a smile as nerves bit at his skin like a legion of red ants.

She stepped closer, eliminating the distance between them, and her warmth mingled with his own. "You look nervous." Her voice was soft, almost teasing, as it reverberated through the quiet room.

A breathy laugh escaped, and as he lifted a shoulder, the fabric of his shirt brushed against his skin. He licked his lips, tasting the lingering sweat from the sparring match. "I'm not very experienced. So, yeah, I am just a little." His voice wavered, betraying his attempts to sound casual. He discreetly rubbed his damp palms against his leathers, trying to steady his trembling hands.

She put her hand over his heart, and her eyes melted with his honesty. "I don't have that much experience either," she admitted, her voice a gentle whisper that seemed to wrap around him like a tender embrace.

The heat of her touch sent a spine-dithering thrill down his back, and his crazed heart quickened beneath her palm. His breath caught in his throat, and he struggled to maintain eye contact, his cheeks flushing with exhilaration. Her words resonated deeply within him. A wave of relief washed over him, easing the tension that had gripped him moments before. The intimate connection between them grew stronger, and he leaned into her touch, savoring the moment as his pulse synchronized with hers.

Their restraint snapped at the same moment, and they collided in a kiss that shed the breath from his chest. Her soft lips glided over his, and her tongue tangled in a dance that had him tearing at the clasps of her armor. She pawed at him with the same urgency, guiding him toward her washroom as their armor and clothing fell in scattered heaps.

Jenna guided him into her bathroom, and Caelum broke the kiss and glanced around at her sleek, modern lavatory as he slipped his boots off. He whistled, impressed by the layout and the ceiling-mounted rain showerhead that promised an entirely unique experience from the rustic soaking tub he was accustomed to. Before he could ask her how it worked, she yanked him into the stall with her.

She turned the knob on the back wall and water cascaded down in a gentle, enveloping flow, almost like standing under a soft, warm rain. He hesitated for a moment, letting the water trickle through his fingers, marveling at the sensation, and he grinned at her. The soothing warmth had his eyelids dropping closed as he surrendered to the unfamiliar but delightful experience.

"This is heaven," he whispered, letting the water loosen his weary muscles. The warmth wrapped around him like a comforting embrace, easing every ounce of tension from his body. Steam rose around them like a gentle mist, softening the harshness of the day. "I'm never leaving your bathroom," he added with a contented sigh, a smile pulling at the edges of his lips. The aroma of lavender filled the air, merging with the sound of the water cascading down his back, creating a serene symphony that lulled him into pure bliss. His hands slipped down her shoulders, and he pulled her to his bare chest. He opened his eyes and met her amused gaze.

"You've never taken a shower before?"

Her teasing grin sparked the fire inside him. Instead of answering, he kissed her again, tasting her lips before he moved to the crook of her neck and licked a trail to her ear. "Can't say as I have."

He spied a bar of soap on a nearby shelf and grabbed it, running the sweet lavender scent over her body, the suds glistening on her skin as they rid her of all traces of dirt from the sparring field. The warm water cascaded around them, creating a soothing symphony of droplets. Her eyes fluttered closed. A soft sigh escaped her lips as she leaned into his touch, the tension melting away with each gentle stroke.

There was something undeniably sexy and intimate about washing the woman he craved, and Caelum never wanted this to end. The tingle of her skin against his fingers left him on the edge of a precipice that he could easily jump into. Each stroke fanned the flames into a burning desire.

When he reached to put the soap back on the shelf, she gently grabbed his wrist and tsked him, a playful glint in her eyes. "My turn," she purred, taking the soap from his hand.

"Oh, by all means." Her feather-light touch lingered on his skin. As she lathered the soap, the silky suds between her fingers, he couldn't help but notice the way the steam swirled around them, creating an intimate cocoon that made everything outside disappear. The sound of the water, the soft rustling of their movements, and the steady rhythm of their breathing blended in perfect harmony. He had thought the shower itself was heaven, but the gentle glide of her hands running over every inch of his skin went beyond all expectations. It nearly undid him.

When she put the soap back and dropped to her knees, he groaned at the image of his goddess sliding her mouth over the tip of his throbbing member. Caelum threaded his fingers through her wet hair, pushing it away from her face as the water rained down around them. Her delicious strokes sent a flurry of emotions through him, creating a pool of heat in his lower belly.

"Fuck, Jenna." His hoarse whisper tilted her lips in a smile as she met his gaze and nearly swallowed him whole in a deliberately slow crawl.

His fingers tightened in her hair. Hell, every muscle tightened with anticipation as she sucked her way to his tip. A purr of approval rumbled in his throat, and although he wanted to tilt his head back and close his eyes from the intensity of this moment, he kept his eyes on her and the magic her mouth was creating at a cellular level.

She twirled her tongue around his sensitive tip. "Come for me, Caelum."

*Oh fuck, she didn't.* The fragmented thought barreled through his head as his body trembled against the need to obey her request. He pushed his hips deep, hitting the back of her throat. The sensation shot liquid heat from his balls through his entire form, and he roared with his release. The sound echoed in the bathroom.

She pulled away with a smirk, the corners of her lips curling upward. As the water cascaded down her face in a cool, refreshing stream, she leaned back and let the droplets splash onto her skin. The rhythmic sound of the water hitting her body created a soothing symphony. With a graceful tilt of her head, she filled her mouth, the liquid swirling around like a refreshing torrent. After a moment, she rinsed and spat, the water splattering on the floor with a satisfying splash. Finally, she stood, droplets of water tracing paths down her skin, glistening under the light.

His body trembled with aftershocks, and he wrapped her in his arms, kissing her tenderly and holding her close as if she were his anchor. She reached over and hit the off button on the shower; the water stopped abruptly, sending shivers nipping at his spine through his overheated skin. The air grew chilly, causing goose bumps to rise on their damp skin.

Her generosity would not be ignored. With determination to hear her moan his name, he swept her off her feet, cradling her against his chest, and headed out of the bathroom. She giggled, a sound that seemed to warm the very air around them, and then pointed toward her room.

Leaving a trail of wet footprints on the polished wood floor, he carried her to the bedroom, their laughter echoing softly in the hallway. The scent of her favorite lavender soap floated in the air, joining with the fresh aroma of clean linens. He gently laid her down on the bed, his gaze never leaving hers, committing every detail to memory.

The world outside seemed to pause, granting them a moment suspended in time. The soft rustling of leaves and the distant chirping of birds created a gentle symphony, wrapping them in a cocoon of stillness. But it shattered abruptly with a brisk knock at the door, echoing through the tiny cottage like a thunderclap.

Caelum stilled, his heart drumming in his chest. Meeting Jenna's gaze, her eyes widened with alarm.

"Jenna?" a familiar female voice called out, cutting through the silence like a knife.

His breath caught in his throat as the reality of the situation set in.

"Your sister," Jenna whispered.

He rolled off her, his movements hurried but silent. The urgency in his voice was clear as he whispered, "Our clothes are in the hall."

Jenna chuckled softly, the sound barely more than a breath. "Your clothes are," she teased, opening a drawer and pulling out a fresh pair of undergarments. She slipped them on with a playful grin, clearly enjoying the moment.

Caelum raked his hand through his hair and shot her a look that clearly conveyed his lack of appreciation for her humor. "I can't go out there like this," he hissed, gesturing wildly at his obvious arousal.

Jenna snorted a laugh, unable to contain her amusement. "Raincheck?" She glanced at the bed and then back at him as she grabbed a clean uniform. With a swift motion, she slid it on, the fabric making a soft, rustling sound.

Heat brushed his cheeks, and he nodded, attempting to regain his composure. "You can bet on it," he muttered, a hint of a smile playing on his lips.

The knock came again, more insistent this time, rattling the door in its frame.

"I'm coming," Jenna called out, her voice calm and steady. She crossed to him and gave him a quick peck on the lips before twirling her wet hair into a messy bun. With a mischievous finger wave, she left the bedroom, leaving him to deal with his predicament.

A moment later, the front door clicked open and closed just as quickly, and the murmurs from outside the house faded into a low hum.

LANAE GAVE JENNA A once-over as she stepped out of her cottage and closed the door in a hurry. Jenna's face was flushed, and her hair was hastily twisted into a messy bun, damp tendrils escaping around her face. The fresh scent of soap wafted from her, mingling with the earthy aroma of the surrounding woods.

"Sorry, I was just cleaning up," Jenna said, out of breath.

Lanae raised an eyebrow, a knowing smile playing on her lips. "It's all right," she replied, her eyes twinkling with amusement. "Ready to head back to the Citadel?"

Jenna nodded, smoothing her uniform and adjusting her hair one last time. They set off down the narrow path leading away from the cottage. The path was lined with tall, ancient trees that cast long shadows over them, and the air was filled with the earthy scent of the forest, mingling with the fresh aroma of pine. The soft crunch of their footsteps on the gravel path added a rhythmic undertone to their walk.

As they strolled toward the barracks, Lanae couldn't help but notice the subtle smile playing on Jenna's lips. "What's got you so amused?" Lanae asked, her tone light and teasing.

"Just thinking about how much of a mess Nero made this morning," Jenna replied, her voice carrying a hint of laughter.

"Nero?" Lanae raised an eyebrow.

"He brought another cow to the training grounds," Jenna explained, her eyes twinkling with amusement.

Lanae sighed and wiped her forehead. "That beast is going to be the death of me."

Jenna laughed, the sound like a musical note blending with the ambient forest noises. "Caelum handled it. Although he's not exactly used to being caught off guard."

"Yeah, he doesn't like surprises," Lanae agreed, her curiosity piqued by the way Jenna grinned. "Care to explain that grin?"

Jenna blushed but managed to keep her composure. "Not really." Her attempt to sound casual failed.

Lanae raised an eyebrow, a sly smile playing on her lips. She had seen the way Jenna and Caelum looked at each other, the unspoken connection between them. "Was Caelum with you in the cottage today?" she asked, her tone dripping with playful curiosity.

Jenna's eyes darted away, her cheeks flushing an even deeper shade of red. "Why do you ask?" she replied, her voice wavering.

Lanae chuckled softly, enjoying the moment. "Oh, no reason. Just curious if he was lending a hand with the 'cleaning up,'" she teased, putting air quotes around the last two words.

Jenna bit her lip, trying to suppress a smile. "Lanae, you're impossible," she muttered, her fingers nervously fidgeting with the hem of her uniform.

Lanae wasn't about to let her off the hook that easily. "Come on, Jenna. Spill the beans. Was he there or not?" she pressed, her eyes sparkling with mischief.

Jenna shifted uncomfortably, her gaze still avoiding Lanae's. She let out a resigned sigh. "All right, fine. Yes, he was with me," she admitted.

Lanae's grin widened, a triumphant gleam in her eyes. "I knew it! So, how was it?"

Jenna couldn't help but laugh at the absurdity of the situation. "It was...nice," she replied, a shy smile curving her lips. "We just talked and...well, you know."

Lanae's expression softened as she reached out and gently squeezed Jenna's shoulder. "I'm glad to hear it." She infused her voice with as much sincerity and warmth as she could. "You two make a good team, both on and off the field." The subtle scent of pine mingled with the distant hum of activity from the Citadel, creating a peaceful backdrop to their conversation.

Jenna's smile faded, her gaze dropping to the ground. "Thanks, but you know it's forbidden, Lanae." Her voice thickened with frustration.

Lanae's lips curved into a knowing smile as she shrugged, her eyes twinkling with mischief. "So was me marrying Draven," she replied, her tone light and playful. She was genuinely happy for her brother and his choice in Jenna, despite the challenges they would face.

She studied Jenna's contemplative expression, noticing how her brows furrowed and her eyes seemed to search for answers in an invisible distance. "It's only worth it if what you have is precious enough to fight for."

Jenna glanced up at Lanae; the flicker of uncertainty in her eyes sent Lanae's heart plummeting.

Lanae paused, considering the situation. Her mind raced through memories of her little brother—the laughter, the arguments, the hurt he experienced after his first infatuation. She gulped down a steadying breath, and her heart gave a kick. "Would you fight for him?"

Jenna's lips parted, as if to speak, but no words came. She swallowed hard, the decision settling heavily on her shoulders.

The road closed in around her as though the very air around them was holding its breath along with her as she awaited Jenna's answer.

# CHAPTER TWELVE
## *Spy Network*

INSTEAD OF GOING HOME after the disastrous council meeting, Draven peeled off from Lanae once she got to Jenna's neighborhood and headed to Mystic Spirits, hoping to settle his burning aggravation with a stiff drink. The narrow streets were bustling with daytime activity, the sun's rays casting a warm glow on the wet pavement that still shimmered from an early morning dew. The scent of fresh rain mixed with the earthy aroma of blooming flowers from the nearby market, filling the air with a refreshing fragrance.

As Draven approached Mystic Spirits, the sounds of conversation and clinking glasses spilled out into the street. He pushed open the heavy wooden door, the hinges creaking as he stepped inside. The bar was filled with natural light streaming through large windows, illuminating the dark, polished wood and casting playful patterns across the room.

Draven made his way to the bar, his boots tapping softly against the worn floorboards. He nodded to the bartender, a burly man with a mane of graying hair, and ordered a stiff drink. As he waited, he scanned the room, searching for a familiar face. The indistinct murmur of voices and the occasional burst of laughter created a lively atmosphere, but his gaze remained sharp and focused.

Just as he took his first sip, savoring the burn of the alcohol as it slid down his throat, he spotted Varkir in a shadowed corner, hunched over a table. The spy's nearly clear eyes met Draven's, and with a subtle nod, Varkir beckoned him over. Draven could see the flicker of unease in Varkir's gaze, a sure sign that he had valuable information to share.

Draven approached, his curiosity piqued. Aged wood and spiced cologne filled the air. "Got something for me, Varkir?" His voice was barely audible above the ambient noise of clinking glasses and hushed conversations.

Varkir leaned in, his breath carrying a hint of mint as he spoke in a conspiratorial whisper. "Our spy network isn't the only one in Solstice City."

Draven's grip tightened around his glass, the cool surface pressing into his skin, the anticipation mingling with his lingering frustration. "I'm listening," he replied, his focus entirely on the spy's next words.

"My sources tell me that Alestain Firetwill is working on a portal potion that can rip open the realms and let an army through."

Draven's jaw clenched, the news aligning with what Lanae had said. But she had destroyed all the vials before she came back. He gave a slow nod for Varkir to continue.

"They are using the Dragon's Heart."

Draven tilted his head, his eyes narrowing as he stared at Varkir. "I thought you told me the Dragon's Heart held no power?"

Varkir shifted in his seat, the wooden chair creaking under his weight. "It doesn't, per se." He bit his lip, glancing around to ensure they weren't overheard. "It seems if they chip off pieces and turn them into liquid, it allows them to add it to the portal potion ingredients they have and it magnifies it by a thousandfold."

Draven pinched the bridge of his nose as the tension mounted. "So, they are destroying the stone?"

Varkir shrugged, his expression one of resignation. "Alestain is chipping small pieces off for their use."

A low rumble of discontent came from Draven, and he took a larger sip of the drink, relishing the way it burned going down his throat, the warmth spreading through his chest. "Anything on that document you mentioned?"

Varkir pulled a parchment out from his cloak and handed it to Draven. The texture of the aged paper was rough against Draven's fingers. "I'd wait until you are home to read that," Varkir said. "And one other thing. There seems to be a spy within the city that is feeding Alestain information on the troops."

Draven clenched his teeth. "Do we know how they are communicating?" His voice carried the sharp edge of frustration.

Varkir shook his head, his movements slow and deliberate. "My sources don't know who it is or how they are communicating. Just that they are." His features scrunched into frustration, his brow furrowing deeply, mirroring the tightness in Draven's expression. The dim light cast shadows on Varkir's face, highlighting the lines of concern etched into his skin. The air charged thick with tension, and uncertainty hung heavy in the space they shared.

Draven attempted to piece together what Varkir was trying to relay, and something did not add up. "Who told you this?" he demanded, casting a glare at Varkir, his ire increasing at the holes in the information. His eyes burned with intensity, the frustration clear in the tense set of his shoulders.

Varkir shut his mouth and closed his eyes, taking a deep breath. "My source is questionable," he admitted.

Smoke bled from Draven's nostrils, a visual manifestation of his rising anger. "Then why did you even bother to tell me this information?" he growled, slashing a glare at Varkir. His voice cut through the ambient noise of the bar.

"Because...if I didn't and it is credible, you'll have my head," Varkir responded, his tone tinged with fear.

He wasn't wrong. Draven took a breath and calmed the rising inferno in his chest. The heat dissipated with each measured inhale. "Take me to this source," he ordered, his voice steady but firm. He had allowed Varkir to run the network since they came back from Xoltan's castle free of Firetwill's mind control.

"Draven," Varkir started in a tone that screamed impossible. The desperation in his eyes was unmistakable.

"I have given you my trust in merging our spy networks. And this is the first time you've given me unreliable information. Why?" Draven's voice was laced with disappointment, his eyes boring into Varkir.

Varkir wiped his face, the frustration evident in the furrow of his brow. "As I said..."

"Don't give me that bullshit," Draven snapped, his patience wearing thin.

Varkir dropped his lids and grumbled as he hung his head. When he glanced up at Draven, his jaw tightened with resolve. "I can feel someone reaching out to Firetwill's realm. I just can't tell you who," he admitted, his voice heavy with the revelation.

Draven's eyes narrowed. "You? You're the unreliable source?" he questioned, his tone laced with disbelief.

"Yes," Varkir replied, his voice a strained whisper, the admission hanging heavily in the air.

Draven studied him, his piercing gaze searching for any hint of deception. "Explain," he demanded as his pulse quickened.

Varkir took a deep breath, his eyes reflecting a hint of terror. "I sense the echo of the call since the mind-controlled have awakened. I was under the blood curse for a long time, Draven." His voice wavered.

The stinging reek of fear burned Draven's nose, mingling with the ambient aromas of the bar.

"The pull of Xoltan's realm has fluctuated over the last couple of days, as if a communications channel has opened or portals have opened." Varkir let out a half laugh, devoid of humor. "At least I recognize the sensation and have been able to ignore the call to arms." He stared at the bottom of his drink as if it held answers he couldn't decipher, his fingers tracing the rim of the glass.

Draven's heart calmed as he processed the information. "Portals have been opening and closing," he stated, the realization settling in.

Varkir's gaze jumped to meet his, a flicker of fright reflected in his pale irises.

"Alestain's son has been here at least twice. He had the balls to kidnap Lanae and then try to pass his shape-shifting ass off as her." Draven's jaw clenched in anger.

Varkir's eyebrows shot up, and he leaned back in his chair, the wood creaking under his weight. "Why didn't you tell me that when we last met?" he demanded, his eyes widening in surprise.

"All of this shit has gone down since we last met," Draven replied, finishing his drink with a final, decisive gulp. The burn of the alcohol lingered in his throat. "Have you felt anything since last night?"

Varkir closed his eyes, his face tightening in concentration. After a few moments, he shook his head, the movement slow and deliberate. "Not since the early evening," he murmured, the frustration evident in his voice.

Draven reached into his cloak and pulled out the only vial left of Firetwill's batch, the green liquid shimmering under the pale glimmer. "I need this analyzed. Who should I go to?" he asked, spinning the clear canister in his fingers.

"May I?" Varkir held out his hand, and Draven offered him the smooth, cool glass. "Where did you get this?" His eyebrows cocked with curiosity and concern.

"Lanae grabbed three of them before she destroyed the rest that were lined up on a table in Firetwill's lab," Draven explained with a shrug. "She used one to get back."

"And where are the others?" Varkir's gaze intensified.

"She lost one in a wrestling match with Alestain's son." Draven pointed to the vial in Varkir's hand. "That is the last one."

"The best sprite I know who dabbles in portal potions is Jairamon. He guards the Isle of Dreams between his laboratory stints," Varkir said, his voice steady and assured.

Draven's chest rumbled with a deep growl. "He sold us a portal potion when we were trying to get Lanae out of the Citadel dungeons," he recalled, the memory flooding back with vivid clarity.

"While I know you can find the Isle of Dreams on your own, I can lead you to his laboratory, since I have some business I need to discuss with the sprite."

Draven nodded, and Varkir handed the jar with the green liquid back to him.

The two rose from their seats, the bar's ambient noise fading into the background as they focused on their next move. The cool metal of the vial in his hand reflected the light, casting small, shimmering glints around the room as they crossed to the door.

Outside, the sun was high in the sky, its rays casting a warm glow over the bustling streets. The scent of fresh rain still drifted on the air, interwoven with the fragrant aroma of blooming flowers and the city's earthy odor. Draven and Varkir moved swiftly, their footsteps echoing on the cobblestones as they headed toward the edge of the city.

The journey to the Isle of Dreams required a trek through the forest outside the city walls. A trek Draven barely remembered. The last time he crossed this way was with Caelum and Nero, looking for the magic to open Nero up to his ancestral powers. That had been one of the quests Varkir had sent him on while Lanae rotted in the Citadel dungeons. One that made it possible for them to beat Xoltan.

The towering trees formed a canopy overhead, their leaves rustling softly in the breeze. Shafts of sunlight pierced through the foliage, creating a dappled pattern of light and shadow on the forest floor. The air was filled with the sweet scent of wildflowers and the distant calls of unseen creatures.

Draven scanned the surroundings for any signs of danger. The forest was alive with subtle sounds—the whisper of leaves, the chirping of birds, and the occasional snap of a twig underfoot. Varkir walked beside him, the tension between them clear in their synchronized, purposeful strides.

As they closed the distance to the cavern that led down to the Isle of Dreams, the fog he remembered rolled like a living beast. It flickered and pulsed, casting an otherworldly glow on the surrounding trees. The path down was just as harrowing as he remembered, but without Jairamon guiding them, the climb was slower and more treacherous. They took care to place their feet on the slippery mud and shifting rock, cursing as the fog thickened around them.

When they reached the bottom of the ravine, the fog cleared, revealing a clearing covered in soft moss that glowed with a gentle, ethereal light. A lazy river cut through the ground, breaking up the lush land with a vein of bright blue, as if the water came from glaciers in the far north. The stream carved a path around an island of moss, and the familiar hum pulsed with rhythmic energy through Draven. Golden coins still littered both the water and the moss. There was more than he recalled, and his dragon growled in want. The shiny objects represented wishes of those who came to request wealth, health, or myriad things from this mystical relic.

Varkir led him beyond the Isle of Dreams and into a clearing. On the other side, a serene landscape of rolling hills lay beyond, with crystalline lakes and vibrant, dreamlike flora. A small, ivy-covered stone building that exuded an air of ancient wisdom sat in the valley.

As they approached, a sprite appeared at the doorway, his iridescent wings catching the light and creating a cascade of colors around him.

"Draven, Varkir," Jairamon greeted them, his voice melodic and welcoming. "What brings you to my isle?"

Draven held up the vial, the green liquid shimmering within. "We need your expertise, Jairamon. Can you analyze this?"

Jairamon took the glass vial and stared at the green shimmer of the liquid, the sunlight catching and refracting within it. "It looks like the same portal potion that I had given you to return to Solstice City." He uncorked it and took a cautious whiff. His brow creased, and he beckoned them inside with a swift gesture.

Draven stared at the door and raised an eyebrow, his broad shoulders tensing. He would never fit through the opening, never mind be able to stand up in the building. "You go," he said to Varkir, his voice a low rumble. After all, the man could become smoke.

And that is exactly what Varkir did. His form dissolved into a wispy, smoky tendril and slithered inside the house.

Jairamon stopped in the doorway. "I'll open the window so you can hear what we say." Jairamon met Draven's hard stare with a resolute nod.

"Thank you," Draven replied, his voice edged with impatience.

Jairamon stepped inside, and a window creaked open, allowing Draven to hear the conversation within.

The air drifting from the window held the scent of herbs and potions. Jairamon moved to a wooden table cluttered with alchemical tools and carefully set down the vial. "This potion...it's not just mine," he murmured, his fingers lightly tracing the glass. "There's something else in here."

Varkir reformed into his solid state, his brows furrowing. "What do you mean, something else?" His voice rose with suspicion. "Have you ever sold your recipe?"

Jairamon's wings fluttered in agitation, the colorful light scattering around the room. "I have never sold my recipe, Varkir. It is my creation, guarded closely."

"Then how did this unknown substance get into the potion?" Varkir pressed, his frustration mounting. "Who could have had access to your ingredients?"

Jairamon's eyes flashed with annoyance, his voice growing sharper. "Are you accusing me of incompetence? I know my own potions. This substance—it's not something I would ever use."

Varkir stepped forward, his posture tense, his shadow stretching across the room. "I'm not accusing you, but we need answers. This is serious. If someone else knows your recipe, they could be dangerous. We need to find out who and how."

Jairamon breathed slowly, visibly trying to calm himself. The ambient sounds of the valley outside amplified the tension between them. "I understand the critical nature of the situation. I will help you identify this substance. But I assure you, my recipe has not been compromised."

Draven watched the exchange through the small, ivy-framed window, his eyes narrowing with intensity. "Let's focus on analyzing the potion first. We can worry about the origins later," he interjected, his voice steady and commanding, carrying authority.

Jairamon nodded, his iridescent wings settling back into a calmer rhythm. "Very well. We will sort this out."

Jairamon went to his workstation, the air filled with the scents of various herbs and potions. He opened one of the intricate contraptions, its brass gears clicking softly. Carefully, he poured a single drop of the green liquid from the vial before recapping it. He moved a scope over the contraption and stared into it, his fingers deftly adjusting the focus. As he muttered to himself, taking meticulous notes, the soft glow of the laboratory's lanterns cast a warm, golden light over the scene.

Draven stared through the tiny window as a cool breeze brushed against his face. He exchanged a glance with Varkir, who lifted a shoulder in a nonchalant shrug. They both returned their gazes to the little sprite, waiting with bated breath.

After a few minutes, Jairamon pulled away from the machine and sent a curious glance up at Draven. "This is my recipe, but modified with something I have never seen." His eyes reflected a mix of confusion and intrigue.

"How many vials have you sold?" Draven's question rumbled through the room, causing all the glass to rattle, the vibrations echoing in the small space.

"Too many to count. Selling potions is my business," Jairamon scoffed, his tone defensive. He looked into the contraption again, his brow furrowing deeper. "It looks like blood was mixed in with my portal potion. But not fae blood," he added with a hint of concern.

The rhythmic hum of the laboratory's machinery and the distant chirping of birds outside were the only sounds that broke the silence.

*Dragon blood.* The thought pierced Draven's mind like an icy dagger. His heart pounded in his chest, each beat echoing with the revelation. The implications were staggering, and an icy dread settled in his stomach. He needed to get home to read whatever was on the parchment tucked in his pocket. If the Dragon's Heart still had traces of dragon blood, Alestain had the power to cross realms just like Draven.

# CHAPTER THIRTEEN
## *Desperate Measures*

LANAE TRUDGED HOME FROM the Citadel after a long day of standing guard, the creak of her armor reminding her of the battles she fought, both on and off the field. The cool evening breeze brushed against her face, carrying with it the scent of blooming moonflowers. She was lost in thought when Caelum sidled up next to her at the intersection of the cobblestone roads at the edge of their neighborhood. The cobblestones were slick with evening dew, dulling the echoes of their footsteps in the stillness.

"Hey, Lanae." He kept pace with her. His presence was a comforting contrast to the chill in the air. He slowed as they edged closer to the house, his expression dropping into trepidation. "We should try to reach them again." He nodded toward the side of the house where their parents' bedroom was.

Lanae sighed and nodded, her heart heavy with uncertainty. "I'm not sure it will do any good."

"We can't give up on them." Caelum shot her a determined look as they advanced toward the house, the gravel crunching under their boots.

Caelum had always been the one with the sunnier outlook. And she smiled at the hope lit in his eyes, especially after the last harrowing encounter they had with their parents.

The blooming moonflowers climbing up the front walls of their home let off a sweet, intoxicating scent as they approached their walkway, their petals glowing softly in the moonlight.

Caelum paused outside the front door, his hand on the handle. "Oh. I almost forgot. Nero slaughtered another cow today."

Lanae tilted her head back in defeat and groaned. "Just what I needed today." She marched through the house to the back door and swung it open, the hinges creaking. Nero pecked at a partially picked carcass, the cold metallic essence of blood blending with the garden's earthy fragrance. "What did you do?"

Nero had the sense to bow his head in shame, but the way his eyes tilted up to look at her made his supplication even more mocking. He lifted a talon and dropped a handful of gold coins at her feet, the clinking sound filling the silence.

"You think that will buy you goodwill from the farmer you stole that beast from?" She swiped the coins into her hand and counted them out.

Although her words had been scolding, the sum he brought back would more than make up for a lost cow. But it was the principle of the matter.

Caelum rubbed the back of his neck and sighed. "I already reamed him on the training field. I think he's restless from the stress that we've all been under lately."

"You stay put. I don't want you flying off unattended again. Understand?" Lanae pointed at the griffin with a stiff finger, her tone firm.

Nero nodded slowly and then dipped his head back to his gruesome meal, the sounds of tearing flesh filling the air.

Lanae sighed, knowing that their bond with Nero was as much a source of strength as it was a challenge. She closed the back door and looked toward their parents' bedroom. "We'll deal with Nero later. Right now, we have more pressing matters."

Caelum grumbled and went about fixing a small tray of food for their parents, the clinking of dishes breaking the stillness.

Lanae needed to lighten the dark mood that blanketed the two of them. A playful smirk pulled at her lips, and she couldn't resist commenting on his earlier escapades. "Speaking of pressing matters, did I interrupt another 'meeting' with Jenna?"

Caelum's cheeks flushed. "Maybe," he admitted as he balanced the tray on his hand. "She invited me to her house after I reprimanded Nero."

"And how did that go?" Lanae raised an eyebrow.

"Um... I think I'm in love with her, Lanae," Caelum said softly, his voice filled with a hopeful fear.

Lanae's expression softened, but she couldn't hide her concern, especially after her conversation with Jenna earlier. "Just be careful, Caelum. You know the laws. If Jenna isn't willing to fight against them, you might end up with a broken heart."

"I know," Caelum replied, his voice filled with determination. "But I have to try. She's worth it."

She turned her attention to the bedroom door and gathered her resolve. Tonight would be different. It had to be.

They moved cautiously to the bedroom where their parents were held captive. Lanae's hands trembled as she slid the key into the lock and grasped the doorknob, pushing it open with a creak. The room was dark, shadows dancing across the walls. The stale odor of confinement filled her senses.

"Mom? Dad?" Caelum called out.

In an instant, their parents lunged at them from the shadows, knocking the contents of the tray over as they ambushed both Lanae and Caelum. Their attack knocked both Lanae and Caelum on their backs as their parents held broken glass to their throats. Lanae's heart clanged in her chest, her breath quick and shallow. The glazed, empty look in her parents' eyes hit like a sword in her midsection, reflecting the control that gripped their minds and the morbid possibility of death at their hands.

"Please, fight it!" Lanae cried out, tears welling in her eyes as she stared up into her mother's blank eyes. "It's us, your children. Remember us!"

Her mother's face contorted with confusion.

Lanae's heart ached, seeing the torment they were in. "Mom, Dad, you must break free," she pleaded, her voice breaking. "We need you."

Caelum lay still with his hands out at his side, staring at their father. His terror echoed in her mind as well as carved into his features. Pain at the rejection accompanied the mind-bending fear. "Please, Dad. Don't." His voice cracked, and a tear slipped out of his eye.

For a moment, their parents' eyes flickered with recognition. They recoiled from both of them, shooting to their feet with abject horror written on their faces. The shards of glass fell from their grip, clattering to the floor. But in a fleeting blink, the mental barrier slammed down, the mind control too deeply rooted.

A shaky sob rose in Lanae's throat as her parents' faces twisted in agony. The struggle was intense, a battle fought within their minds. Lanae climbed up on shaky feet and stepped toward them, reaching out in hopes she could touch the part of them that still remembered love.

But the control tightened its grip, and their parents' eyes glazed over once more. They hesitated as their features twisted into hateful glares, and they made a sudden dash for the door.

Caelum scrambled to his feet, and they leaped for the door before it slammed shut, but their parents were faster. The scraping of the lock being engaged echoed in the dark room.

Caelum tried the doorknob, and it didn't move in his hand. "They trapped us in here." Caelum banged on the door. "Let us out, now."

The only sound that came through was the slam of the front door.

Lanae crossed to the window in time to see two figures slinking through the shadows and slipping out of sight.

"Nero!" Caelum shouted, hoping the griffin would hear them.

From outside, Nero let out a savage cry and hopped over the fence in the back. He approached the window and beat his powerful wings against the wall, the sound like thunder against the night.

"Go get Draven," Lanae ordered.

Lanae and Caelum exchanged a grim look. Their parents had escaped, but at what cost?

As the darkness enveloped them, they held onto the faint glimmer of hope that still burned within their hearts. Together, they would face whatever challenges lay ahead, united in their relentless pursuit to free their parents from the chains that bound them.

DRAVEN MOPPED THE SWEAT from his forehead. His hand trembled as the sprite continued to examine the glowing potion. The laboratory was filled with the acrid odor of burning herbs and the soft hum of arcane energy. The thick and oppressive air weighed on Draven's shoulders.

The sudden beat of wings captured Draven's attention, and he looked up to see Nero diving from the sky, his majestic feathers glinting in the dim light. The griffin landed gracefully next to Draven, his talons digging into the earth with a soft thud. Nero cawed, pawing at the ground with a sense of agitation.

The griffin grabbed the hem of Draven's sleeve with his beak and pulled, his golden eyes filled with urgency.

A flare of anxiety coursed through him, and his heart ran amok in his chest. He turned to the small, grimy window and called out, "Varkir, I need to go."

Varkir met his gaze, his expression inscrutable. "I'll find you once Jairamon is done here," he replied, his voice a whisper against the backdrop of the bubbling potions.

Draven marched away from the sprite's laboratory, the chill of the night air biting at his skin. The sky was painted in deep hues of indigo and violet, with stars scattered like diamonds. It was late enough for both Caelum and Lanae to be home, probably preparing dinner.

"Home?" Draven asked the griffin, and Nero responded with an emphatic nod, his feathers rustling.

Draven spoke the ancient draconian spell that called his portal magic to the surface. The familiar warmth spread through his veins. The air around them shimmered and shifted, distorting the world for a moment. He reached out and grabbed a handful of the griffin's soft scruff, and they stepped through the portal together, emerging in the familiar confines of the living room.

The sudden pounding from inside Lanae's parents' bedroom nearly made Draven growl in frustration. The muffled voice that followed sent a jolt of dread through him, pooling in his belly like cold lead. He crossed to the door, his pulse quickening.

The key wasn't on the doorframe, nor was it in the keyhole. The knob resisted his touch, refusing to turn. "Lanae?" he called out, just to be sure.

"Draven, help us," came the desperate reply, muffled yet unmistakable.

"Step back," he yelled, bracing himself. He counted to three in his head. His dragon strength surged to the surface. With a powerful kick near the knob, the entire frame shuddered. "Damn reinforcements," he muttered, his breath coming in quick, frustrated bursts. They had fortified the door to protect against their parents escaping, and now he was paying for their thoroughness.

Determined, he stepped back to the far side of the hall. With a deep breath, he barreled toward the door, leading with his shoulder. The impact sent a pulse of pain radiating through him, but this time, the door groaned in protest. It was giving way, inching closer to rescuing those trapped inside.

With a determined glare, Draven took a step back once more, his shoulders squared and muscles tensed. He let out a frustrated growl, channeling his dragon strength into another powerful kick. The doorframe groaned, but still held firm, mocking his efforts.

"Damn it!" Draven spat, his breath coming in sharp bursts. The urgency of the situation pushed him to the brink.

Nero stood beside him, pacing anxiously and occasionally letting out a worried caw.

Draven pounded the door with his fists, the wood echoing his frustration. The door shuddered under the barrage, but stubbornly refused to yield. "Lanae, hold on!" he yelled, his voice strained with desperation.

His nostrils burned with his lungs' drag of air, his body trembling with exertion. With one final burst of energy, Draven hurled himself at the door, shoulder first. The impact sent a jolt of pain through him, but the door finally splintered and gave way.

Draven stumbled forward, his momentum carrying him into the room. He sprawled out on the floor, the sudden give of the door leaving him momentarily disoriented.

As Draven pushed himself up, the scent of dust and aged wood filled his nostrils. His eyes locked onto Lanae and Caelum, who were huddled together at the farthest point from the door. Relief washed over their faces. The faint, musty odor of the room blended with the lingering aroma of dinner, producing a disorienting olfactory experience.

Nero filled the doorway, his majestic form casting a protective shadow over them. The griffin gave a thankful caw, his feathers ruffling in response.

"Thank you, Nero!" Lanae's voice trembled with gratitude. She crossed the room to Draven, her footsteps echoing softly on the wooden floor. "And thank you for coming so quickly." She placed a whisper of a kiss on his cheek, sending that pleasant jolt of electricity through him, a spark of warmth amidst the chaos.

Draven nodded, still trying to steady his breathing as he wrapped his arm around her. Her warmth seeped into him, providing a brief moment of solace. "What happened?" he asked.

"They attacked us when we brought dinner in," Caelum said, his voice strained. He wiped his throat, his fingers coming away with tacky, dark-red blood.

The metallic scent of it mingled with the other odors, turning Draven's stomach.

Draven lifted Lanae's chin gently, his fingers grazing her soft skin. Anger mounted at the red scratch on her neck, an unwanted reminder of the danger they faced outside the fragile sanctuary of their home.

"We thought we could get through to them." Lanae met his gaze, her eyes reflecting the hurt and devastation that mirrored her brother's. Their shared pain added to the already stifling atmosphere of the room.

Draven's heart pined with the need to protect them, his resolve hardening with each passing moment. The scent of blood and fear lingered.

And now that danger included Lanae and Caelum's parents. The very thought sent a slice of fear skittering down his spine. Icy tendrils wrapped around his heart, making each breath a struggle against the tide of dread. He clenched his fists as the tremor of uncertainty rippled through him.

He shivered at what he might have to do to protect those he loved the most and what it might mean for their future. The image of Lanae's eyes, filled with hurt and devastation, flashed in his mind. He knew he had to be strong for her, for all of them, even if it meant facing the unthinkable.

# CHAPTER FOURTEEN
## *Bitter Truth*

**D**RAVEN DROPPED INTO THE worn leather chair by the fire, its warmth enveloping him like a comforting embrace. The crackling flames cast flickering light dancing across the room. He pulled the parchment Varkir had given him out of his pocket, its texture rough and ancient under his fingertips. He spread the fragile paper on the cocktail table in front of him, the faint aroma of aged parchment mingling with the smoky scent of the fire. He smoothed out the creases, as if that could soften the agitation growing inside his soul.

From the kitchen, the savory scent of dinner being prepared wafted through the air. Lanae and Caelum were busy cooking, the clatter of pots and the sizzle of ingredients providing a backdrop to the evening. His hovering after the scene in their parents' bedroom had irked Lanae enough to shoo him away, her eyes flashing with frustration. None of them mentioned the unspoken truth that now hung heavily between them—her parents, free from captivity, would likely join the enemy side once the war began.

He shook the morbid thought away and focused on the words on the parchment. It had been ages since he had seen the draconian language, and his mind struggled to form the ancient words and their meanings. The faded ink and intricate script seemed to pulse with an almost mystical energy.

"What's that?" Lanae's voice broke through his concentration as she came into the room, wiping her hands on a dish towel. The succulent scent of herbs clung to her, mingling with the odors of the kitchen.

"An ancient parchment that explains the Dragon's Heart," Draven replied, glancing up at her. "Varkir procured it for me." He flipped his eyes back to the paper, its importance pressing down on him.

"Is it authentic?" She stepped closer, her curiosity piqued as she scanned the document. The firelight highlighted the concern etched on her face.

"Yes. This is in draconian." He tapped the foreign language, the rhythmic tapping a faint echo in the room. He glanced up at her.

Lanae's lips pressed together, a frown forming. "What if it's another trick?"

Alestain's brother, Xoltan, had manipulated them before, but Draven knew better. The rich, earthy scent of the parchment filled his senses, grounding him in the moment. Even if their history books had been spared, no one outside the dragons knew draconian. "We never taught the fae our ancestral language."

"Tell me what it says." Lanae moved to the chair opposite him, the flickering firelight radiating on her determined face. She waited, her eyes fixed on Draven with an expectant gaze.

Draven's hand hovered over the parchment, his fingers tracing the ancient script. The warmth of the fire caressed his skin, but it did nothing to ease the chill of uncertainty that settled in his bones. He swallowed hard, his throat dry. "What about dinner?" He nodded toward the kitchen, where the savory aroma of cooking wafted from.

"Caelum's got it," Lanae replied, her voice steady. She cocked her head, as if studying him, her eyes reflecting concern and curiosity.

Draven's pulse quickened, a reluctant thump against his rib cage. The enormity of the parchment's contents pushed down on him. The fire crackled, filling the silence that stretched between them. Hesitation gnawed at him, the fear of what the ancient words might reveal.

His mind raced, grappling with the significance of the Dragon's Heart and the implications it held. The creases on the parchment seemed to deepen, mirroring the furrows of worry on his brow. He inhaled, the scent of old paper mingling with the smoky aroma of the hearth.

Lanae's eyes held her unwavering trust. It was both a comfort and a burden. The flicker of hope in her gaze spurred him to push past his hesitation. He exhaled slowly; the tension eased just a fraction.

"All right." His voice carried a hint of the trepidation throttling his muscles. He read the ancient text, the draconian language rolling off his tongue with a sense of reverence and caution. Each word was heavy with a piece of his destiny.

The more he read, the more sadness flushed his skin, a heavy weight settling on his shoulders. It had been nearly a century since he had heard more than just a few spells spoken in his native language. The ancient draconian words, both foreign and familiar on his tongue, stirred memories long buried. His chest squeezed at the profound sense of loss, each word like a ghost of the past.

When he finished, he stared at the parchment with a lump in his throat. The firelight cast a warm, flickering glow on the delicate script. The room was silent, save for the soft crackling of the fire and the faint clatter of dishes from the kitchen.

"That was beautiful. What does it all mean?" Lanae's voice held reverence, her eyes wide with wonder.

"It means the dragons were the ones who fueled the stone's magic, not the other way around," he replied. His voice carried the bone-deep sorrow accosting him. The parchment seemed fragile in his hands, like the delicate threads of their history. "They annually offered their blood to connect to the stone." He bit his lip. "It was a rite that I had not joined yet. When a dragon turned thirteen, that was when they joined the annual rite." He wiped his face with a trembling hand. Fate had seen that he never experienced that sacred ritual.

Melancholy painted her expression, making her lips pull down at the edges, and her eyes shined with unshed tears. The firelight reflected in her gaze, adding a glimmer of sadness. He looked away from her, swallowing his own tears at all he had missed, the bitter splash of regret lingering in his mouth.

"Once the ritual was completed, the dragon could leverage the power of the community if they needed to. And if the stone ever got into the hands of an enemy, they could wield it against us." He sniffled, the scent of old parchment and burning wood filling his senses. He let out a bitter laugh, the sound hollow in the quiet room. "According to the parchment, if that happened, all the dragons would be killed." Heat ran down his cheeks; a mix of anger and sorrow burned with the path of his tears. "And the Dragon's Heart would never hold power again."

"You don't know that." Lanae's voice carried a fragile thread of hope.

He tapped the parchment, the sound a sharp contrast to the silence. "Yes, I do. If they stopped the annual blood ritual and the Dragon's Heart's power died, it would take centuries of annual blood rites of the entire clan to spark it back to life. That's hundreds of dragons." He let that sink in. "And there certainly isn't enough blood in a single dragon to resurrect the damned thing."

Lanae reached over and took his hands in hers, her touch warm and reassuring against his cool skin. The soft pressure of her fingers sent a wave of comfort through him, momentarily easing the turmoil in his chest. She gently squeezed in a show of support, her eyes searching his face for answers. "What does this mean for you?" she asked with a voice filled with concern.

He laughed, a hollow sound that did nothing to mask his frustration. Uncertainty pressed down on him as he pulled away from her hands, the warmth slipping away. The worn leather of the chair creaked under his weight as he leaned back. He raked his fingers through his hair. The silky strands slipped through his fingers, tangling as he tried to collect his thoughts.

He had been counting on the Dragon's Heart to give him the power to fully shift, but knowing it was a dead crystal, where did that leave him? The flickering firelight cast shifting shadows on the walls, mirroring the chaotic storm of emotions inside him. The scent of fiery wood filled his nostrils, grounding him in the moment yet reminding him of the burning question that now haunted his mind.

"I don't know." His eyes found solace in hers.

LANAE'S THROAT CLOSED AT the soul-wrenching devastation reflected in Draven's eyes. The certainty that finding the Dragon's Heart would give him the ability to shift lay shattered at their feet, like delicate glass. Her back went ramrod straight as determination to wipe that look away raged through her, a fiery resolve burning in her chest.

"When was the last time you fully shifted?" she asked with a soft edge of fortitude.

His silence unnerved her, a heavy quiet that made her question whether he had ever shifted at all. The seconds stretched on, each one amplifying her anxiety.

"It was the morning of the day our world went to shit," Draven finally replied, his voice a hollow echo of pain and loss.

Relief washed through Lanae, a soothing balm against the raw edges of her worry. He had done it before, so he could do it again—even without the magical crystal. "Tell me about it," she urged, her voice a gentle coaxing.

Pain washed over Draven's face, his features contorting with the memory. "I flew with my older siblings. I was the youngest in the family, and my sister told me I could never beat them in a race. She was quite the brat at times, but I loved her, and I never backed down from a challenge." His lips tilted into a smile, a bittersweet curve that didn't quite reach his eyes. As he spoke, his gaze grew distant, the firelight casting shifting shadows on his face.

He chuckled softly, a sound tinged with nostalgia, and glanced down at his hands, the fire's glow highlighting the creases of his palms. "I finally beat them that day. I was faster than all my older siblings." His smile faded, leaving behind a hollow ache. "My mother looked so proud, but my father just vacantly stared at me and walked away. His lack of any sort of comment hurt, and I went to my room to lick my wounds. My brothers and sister tried to console me, but my mother shooed them outside. If they hadn't gone outside, perhaps they would have survived."

The guilt layered over every word tugged at Lanae's heartstrings. Her own eyes burned with unshed tears. "Oh, Draven."

Draven's vulnerability shut down at the empathy in her voice. He stared at the parchment with his history and loss heavy in his heart. "It was supposed to be an extinction event." His throat bobbed as he swallowed. "Why was I spared?" His question hung in the air, a haunting echo of survivor's guilt.

"Perhaps because fate knew your soulmate wasn't born yet." Lanae offered a kind smile, her eyes softening as she cocked her head to the side.

Draven blinked at her, the flickering shadows reflecting in his eyes. He crossed his arms over his chest, as if shielding himself from her words. "Fate?" he spat out, the word carrying a bitter edge. His eyes shuttered, a spark of fury igniting in their depths.

Lanae lifted her shoulder in a delicate shrug. "I like to think fate knew better than to snuff out your life." She picked at her fingernail, the faint sound just audible above the crackling fire. "If not for you, I would be Xoltan's plaything." The solemnity of her words lingered, reminding them of the dark reality they had overcome together.

Draven grumbled, the sound low and rugged, and rubbed his face with a weary hand. The rough stubble on his jaw rasped against his palm, a physical manifestation of his inner turmoil. "I know. Fate is cruel, but at least she offered you as a gift to soothe my troubled soul." His lips finally tilted into a smile, a fleeting warmth amidst the tension. "Otherwise, I would have had to hunt down that fickle bitch and torch her into ash." The fire's glow highlighted the determined glint in his eyes.

A quick burst of humor fell from Lanae's lips, the sound light and airy. She pressed them together to stifle the laughter. It would be so like Draven to go after a presence like fate. She let the image linger in her head—Draven, fierce and determined, stalking an ethereal being. The thought lit a fire inside her, a flicker of warmth and amusement that momentarily chased away the shadows of their situation.

She had to shake it away and focus on Draven yet again. His presence, solid and grounding, drew her back to reality. "After we eat, we should go down to the training grounds so you can try to shift," she suggested, her voice gentle but firm. The scent of cooking from the kitchen mingled with the scent of smoldering fire, creating a comforting backdrop.

The humorous glint in Draven's eyes faded, replaced by a shadow of worry. "You know my fire gets unstable after attempting to shift." His voice carried a sour note of caution. The fire's glow highlighted the worry lines etched on his forehead, the flickering light casting shifting shadows on his troubled expression.

"What's the worst that could happen?" She tried to keep her tone light, but the underlying concern seeped through.

DRAVEN COULD NOT BELIEVE she even suggested for him to try shifting. She had seen how volatile he was after his partial shift years ago. And for her to say what's the worst thing that could happen? Aggravation built in his core. "I could sneeze and burn this house down. Or hurt you or Caelum or Nero." Draven's voice rumbled with frustration. He rubbed his face, the rough stubble rasping against his fingers.

"Or you could finally push yourself past your mental barrier and shift." Lanae's voice carried a sharp edge, her eyes hardening with determination. She crossed her arms over her chest, the gesture both defensive and challenging.

A surge of frustration welled up inside Draven, like a coiled spring ready to snap. "Mental barrier?" he repeated, his voice low and taut with tension. He ground his teeth together, the muscles in his jaw clenching painfully. The air popped with his unspoken resentment, the flickering firelight casting sharp shadows on her face.

Just as his anger threatened to ignite, Caelum stepped into the room, cutting off the scathing remark poised on his lips.

"Dinner's ready," Caelum announced, the scent of the meal wafting through the air, uniting with the whiff of burned essence of the fire.

Draven tore his gaze away from Lanae. A mix of anger and helplessness churned within him. Her insinuation pressed down on him, a heavy burden he wasn't sure he could bear. His breast swelled with an in-breath as he tried to steady the whirlwind of emotions that threatened to overwhelm him. The warmth of the fire did little to chase away the chill that settled in his bones.

Lanae stood and headed toward the kitchen, her heels clicking sharply against the hardwood floor. The small shake of her head to her brother nearly pulled a smoky growl from Draven, the bitter scent of his frustration filling the air.

"Don't unload my shit to your brother," he snapped, his voice echoing off the walls.

Caelum glanced at him with a hardened expression, the muscles in his jaw tightening. "She wasn't." He stepped in front of Draven as Lanae passed through the kitchen door, stopping him with a palm to his chest. The contact was firm, the warmth of Caelum's hand seeping through Draven's shirt. "Do not speak to her with that tone."

The protective flare in his eyes caused Draven to pause, the intensity almost tangible. He shuttered his gaze and sighed, the tension in his shoulders easing. Caelum had become more than just a little brother-in-law. He had become one of Draven's more level-headed friends. "She wants me to try to shift."

Caelum cocked a single eyebrow, the flicker of curiosity in his eyes. "Really?" He dropped his hand from Draven's chest, the absence of warmth noticeable.

"Yeah," he said.

They walked into the kitchen, where sweet scents of freshly brewed tea and baked bread filled the air. They took their seats at the table with no other conversation, the silence punctuated only by the distant hum of the rune lights.

They ate in tense silence, the clinking of utensils against plates the only sound filling the room.

Caelum's forehead creased halfway through the meal, and he lifted his gaze to Draven. "Is there a reason you shouldn't try?"

"Because partial shifting makes my fire unstable." Draven tried to keep his irritation from his voice, but it seeped through, his jaw tightening with frustration.

Caelum sat back, trading a glance with Lanae, the subtle shift in the air indicating their silent communication. "But what if you find you can fully shift?"

Draven opened his mouth, intent on whipping a snide remark at Caelum, but thought twice and closed it. Caelum wasn't being glib with him and deserved an answer in kind. "I haven't fully shifted since before the dragons fell." The words were bitter on his tongue, a reminder of past failures.

"But—"

Lanae tried to butt in on the conversation, but Caelum held up a hand, cutting his sister off with a calm authority that Draven found both reassuring and irritating. Draven traded a glance with Lanae, then refocused on Caelum, ignoring her rising annoyance with him.

Caelum was the calmer of the two siblings, and curiosity reigned over his questions, not some ticking clock to doom like Lanae's. So, when his head cocked, and he asked, "Can I ask why?" Draven didn't have the instinct to snap. Instead, a flicker of something—respect, perhaps—braised his skin.

"I thought my shifting ability was tied to the Dragon's Heart. But it isn't." Air whizzed over his teeth, bringing a wash of coolness to his lungs, momentarily soothing his agitation. "Your sister thinks I have a mental block that's stopping me."

"Is she right?" Caelum took a sip of his tea, the steam rising in lazy tendrils, while waiting for Draven to answer.

Draven put his silverware down and pushed back his seat. He crossed to the back door and stared out at the picked bones in the yard, the stark-white remnants a grim reminder of Nero's carelessness. He bit his lip, the coppery taste of blood mingling with his thoughts as he considered the possibility of whether Lanae was right. If he had a mental block, he had no idea how to overcome such an obstacle.

His denial of being able to fully shift was ingrained over a century of failed tries. The partial shift in the battle for the gauntlet stone had been the most progress he had made, but there still was a barrier that stopped him.

A chair scraped behind him, breaking his reverie, and a warm hand landed on his shoulder, sending a buzzing calmness through him. He turned and met Lanae's questioning stare, her eyes searching his. Then he looked beyond her at Caelum.

"I don't know." His admission burned in his throat like acid. "If she is, I don't have a clue how to break whatever mental hold is stopping me."

"YOU SHOULD AT LEAST try." Lanae scanned his fearful features, noting the worry in his clenched jaw and the furrow of his brow. Waves of apprehension radiated from him. Wrapping her arms around him, her fingers brushed the tautness of his muscles. "Even if you fail today, we can try again tomorrow and the next day and keep trying until you break through whatever is holding you back."

"But the risks," he started, his voice carrying a rough edge that betrayed his inner turmoil.

She covered his mouth with her hand, and his warm breath tickled her palm. "If I recall, those effects happen when you exhausted yourself." She met his gaze, her eyes locking onto his, searching for the slightest hint of reassurance. "I'll make sure you get your rest."

He positively glowered at that, the fire in his eyes momentarily igniting before he looked away, a muscle ticcing in his jaw. But he didn't turn down the option, and she could sense a sliver of hope piercing through the layers of doubt.

# CHAPTER FIFTEEN
## *Breaking Barriers*

FOR THE THIRD NIGHT in a row, they stood on the empty training ground. Land stretched out before Draven, an expanse of flattened dirt and scattered stones that seemed to whisper both promises of grandeur and humiliation. The scent of freshly turned earth mixed with the crisp evening air, while the soft rustle of leaves created a rhythmic backdrop. Birds watched from the treetops, their curious eyes gleaming like tiny jewels in the shimmering moonlight, eagerly waiting for the comedic spectacle of the evening: Draven the Inept, attempting to shift. Again.

"Lanae," Draven whined, shifting from one foot to the other. The rough grit of dirt crunched beneath his boots. "We've been at this for hours."

Lanae rolled her eyes and traded a glance with Caelum, who leaned against a tree at the sidelines. "It's been thirty minutes, Draven. Now focus. Close your eyes and picture your dragon. Feel him within you."

*Easy for her to say. She wasn't a shifter. She had no clue how this was supposed to happen.* His memories of instruction from when he was little were hazy at best. Over a hundred years had pushed those memories into the recesses of his mind, shrouded in a fog he couldn't penetrate. His dragon seemed to prefer napping or mockingly snorting fire every time he tried.

But it wasn't just that. The deaths of his kin weighed heavily on him, creating a mental block he couldn't seem to break. Survivor's guilt gnawed at his resolve, leaving him in a state of helplessness and unworthiness.

Draven pressed his eyes closed and breathed in the scent of damp earth and pine. He attempted to commune with his inner beast, focusing on the last time his scales had surfaced during the fight for the gauntlet stone. His dragon had taken control, forcing a partial shift. But that had been born of fury and panic.

"Lanae, I can't." He met her gaze, eyes filled with frustration.

"You can." She stepped closer, her scent of lavender and steel enveloping him as she put her hand on his chest, sending that familiar humming spark through him. "Now imagine your dragon, Draven. Feel the shift."

He squeezed his eyes shut again, envisioning scales sprouting, wings unfurling, bones snapping into place. *Wait, was that his stomach growling?* Dinner seemed like it had been hours ago, and frankly, he'd rather shift into a sandwich right now.

Lanae clapped her hands, the sharp sound echoing in the stillness, breaking his feeble concentration. "Draven, you're not even trying!"

"Of course I am!" he protested, the heat of embarrassment flushing his face. "You think I don't want to take to the skies again? That I want to be land-bound and vulnerable?"

She sighed, crossing her arms, the light catching on the white and pink threads of her unbound hair. "You are not vulnerable. You have never been vulnerable. You are a fucking dragon king, a force to be reckoned with. Now act like it."

Her words bolstered his ego, and he took a breath, the crisp air filling his lungs. He tried again. This time, a twinge flared, a small spark of hope. His arms tingled, his chest warmed...and then nothing. Absolutely nothing. His beast roared with displeasure, its fiery breath searing the edges of his consciousness.

"You're overthinking it," Caelum called from the sidelines, his voice smooth and steady. "You need to let go of whatever is holding you back."

*Easy for him to say.* Letting go meant embracing the possibility of becoming a scaly cannonball mid-shift and hurting both Lanae and Caelum in a fiery blast.

Lanae took his face between her hands, her touch cool against his flushed skin, and studied his eyes. "You will not harm us. And it's time to move past your survivor's guilt. You've held onto it long enough." Her determined gaze left no room for argument.

He braced himself, grounding his feet in the loose soil, focusing on the imagined strength of his dragon form. He could almost hear the triumphant roar of success...just before he sneezed a plume of fire and stumbled backward, the heat singeing the air.

"This isn't working, Lanae. Maybe I'm just broken," he said, half-joking, half-defeated, the tinge of ash lingering on his tongue.

She shook her head. "You're not broken. You're just...complicated. Now, breathe. Feel the ground beneath your feet and let the shift come naturally."

Following her guidance, he closed his eyes once more, grounding himself. The world quieted, the ambient sounds fading to a distant hum, and the faintly familiar connection to his dragon brushed his skin. He latched onto it, willing the change.

A sudden warmth enveloped him, the heat radiating from within, and for a brief, glorious moment, he thought he'd done it. Until he opened his eyes to find he'd shifted...into a partially scaled, half-human, half-dragon mess. His dragon slammed against his mental barrier, frantic to be free of his human cage.

Lanae and Caelum burst into laughter, the sound ringing in his ears, and despite himself, Draven joined in. Because really, what else could he do? The heat of embarrassment brushed over his scaled cheeks, a deep crimson.

"Well," he said, trying to keep his balance, "at least I didn't turn into a sandwich."

Lanae wiped away tears of laughter. "Small victories, Draven. Small victories."

The training grounds echoed with their laughter, the evening air carrying the sound into the trees. And even though he hadn't fully shifted, Draven knew he was making progress. Slowly but surely, he'd get there. But he wasn't sure he'd be able to master the change before the war came to their doorstep.

LANAE WAS GIDDY AT the partial transformation. The cool night air carried the scent of pine and earth, mingling with a hint of smoke from Draven's breath. This was the first time in the last three grueling nights he had actually pulled his dragon to the surface. Albeit a partial shift like he had the last time in the throes of war. But a shift all the same.

She launched herself into his scaly arms, the rough texture of his scales cool and firm beneath her fingers. As she pressed kisses on the soft reptilian skin that covered his face, warmth radiated from him.

He jerked away, his eyes wary, the sharp lines of his newly transformed features catching the moonlight.

"Stop being self-conscious. You're a gorgeous beast," she whispered, her breath mingling with his. She kissed him again, this time on the lips. The sharp teeth that lined his mouth grazed her own.

He shuttered his eyes, a low rumble escaping his throat, and the subtle shift of his scales burrowing back under his skin sent tremors down her spine. When his lids opened again, Draven's bright-green irises gazed down at her with an intensity that made her heart race. He returned the kiss, his lips warm and inviting, igniting the familiar warmth in her belly.

"Come on, guys."

Caelum's sharp voice washed his disdain over her, reminding them of their surroundings. Lanae reluctantly pulled away, her eyes still locked with Draven's. The training grounds, once filled with the echoes of their laughter, now appeared charged with their sexual tension. The air seemed to hum with anticipation, the shadows deepening as the night wore on.

Draven's breath came in short bursts, and his eyes searched hers, reflecting the turmoil hiding under the guise of lust.

She peeled herself out of his arms. "We need to keep going," Lanae said. "You were so close, Draven. I know you can do this."

Draven nodded, determination flaring in his eyes. He glanced at Caelum, who stood with arms crossed, his expression unreadable. "All right, let's try again."

This time, the scales came out in seconds, not minutes or hours like before. Her heart leaped inside her rib cage, and she stepped back, giving him room to explore the new form that seemed to stretch the space enclosing his body. She wondered what he would look like as a full-grown dragon. *Would all his scales be the same color, or would they differ?*

A sudden gust of wind swept through the training grounds, carrying the scent of something foreign and dangerous, like the crackling of the ozone itself.

Draven's eyes flew open, and his scales retreated. His gaze scanned the surrounding area.

"Did you feel that?" Lanae asked.

Before Draven could respond, a low growl rumbled from the shadows. The night seemed to hold its breath. The once comforting sounds of the forest were now eerily silent.

"Something's coming," Caelum said.

The three of them stood tense and ready, the training grounds now a stage for an impending confrontation. Lanae's heart pounded in her chest, her body humming with the power of the full moon overhead. Whatever lurked in the darkness, it was about to force their hands in ways they hadn't anticipated.

# CHAPTER SIXTEEN
## *Sacrificial Love*

A PLUME OF BLACK smoke coiled menacingly above the city, a familiar and ominous signal that sent an icy shiver down Draven's spine. Alestain's dark magic. The acrid scent of burning filled the air, stinging Draven's nose as the significance hit him like a tidal wave. His head snapped toward Caelum, eyes wide with urgency. He had no time left to master his shift.

A piercing caw sliced through the tense atmosphere, drawing their gaze skyward. Nero, the griffin, plummeted toward them with eyes blazing like molten gold, mirroring the frantic turmoil within Draven. The surrounding air crackled with the griffin's raw, untamed energy.

"At least he came at a full moon," Lanae remarked, her voice carrying a forced nonchalance that scarcely masked her own anxiety.

Draven let out a bitter huff, his breath visible in the chilly night air. "All fae seem to be strongest at the full moon." His eyes, sharp as a blade's edge, locked onto hers. "Including Alestain."

Lanae's confident demeanor crumbled, her expression shifting to one of dawning dread. Her smug features fell into an unmistakable look of "oh shit." She and Caelum might be stronger tonight, but so were all the fae forces under Alestain's sinister command.

"We need our weapons." Lanae spun to Draven, her voice tight with urgency.

The speedy clip of Draven's heart thundered in his ears as he realized their weapons were across the city, back at their home. The thought of leaving the safety of their position to retrieve them filled him with a sense of dread. He grabbed Lanae's hand, needing her heat to fight against the cold rippling through the air. "Hold on to Nero," he instructed, waving Caelum closer.

He closed his eyes and whispered the draconian portal spell, the ancient words rolling off his tongue like molten lava. The air shimmered and rippled, a gust of wind whipping through their hair. The portal opened with a crackle of energy, revealing the familiar sight of their home, the weapons gleaming on the walls like silent sentinels.

They stepped through the portal, the sensation of being pulled through space disorienting but fleeting. The familiar scent of their home greeted them, a mixture of wood smoke and herbs that calmed Draven's racing heart for a moment. They quickly grabbed their weapons, the cool weight of the steel providing a sense of reassurance and readiness.

With their swords in hand, they stepped outside into the chaos of the city streets. The acrid stench of smoke was even stronger now, mingling with the iron tang of blood and the earthy undertone of freshly turned soil. Shadows danced along the walls as flames flickered in the distance, casting a hellish glow over the chaos that had taken hold of their home.

The sounds of battle assaulted their ears—clashing swords, the shouts of the mind-controlled fae, and the terrified cries of the citizens. Draven's chest pounded in sync with the frenzied rhythm of the conflict. He saw the glint of moonlight on armored figures advancing toward them, eyes vacant and glowing with Alestain's malevolent influence.

"Stay close!" Draven shouted over the racket, his voice a guttural growl that barely reached Lanae and Caelum. The intensity of their determination and fear layered over him as they prepared to face the oncoming wave.

Draven's sword clashed with the first of Alestain's warriors, the impact sending a jolt up his arm. He danced through the chaos with a lethal grace, his movements fueled by a fierce determination. The air around him buzzed with the magic of his enemies, each strike a clash of wills and weapons.

Lanae and Caelum fought at his side, their synchronized efforts a testament to their bond and training. Despite the odds, a sliver of hope remained. If they could hold their ground, if

Draven could push past his mental barriers and fully embrace his dragon form, they just might stand a chance.

CAELUM FOUGHT WITH THE same sense of dread layering over his mind that plagued his sister. With each strike of swords, accompanied by the empty stare of the attackers, they edged closer to their worst nightmare. Magic crackled in the air from all elemental factions on both sides, an overwhelming symphony of power and chaos.

Lanae and Caelum's magic surged through the ground beneath their feet, causing the very earth to tremble with their might. With a swift motion, Lanae summoned thick, twisting vines that erupted from the cobblestones, ensnaring the legs of their enemies and dragging them down with a muted, bone-crunching thud. The rich, loamy scent of freshly turned soil and crushed leaves filled the air, a pronounced opposition to the acrid stench of burning and blood.

Caelum's hands glowed as he called forth jagged spikes of rock from the ground. They shot up with a deep, rumbling growl, impaling the attackers and forming a makeshift barricade. The surrounding ground pulsed in rhythm with their heartbeats and responded to their every command.

Around them, the city was a maelstrom of elemental magic. Fire roared and crackled, its searing heat radiating in waves that singed the vines caging their enemies. The air shimmered with the haze of heat, and the scent of charred wood and sulfur was nearly suffocating. Water magic swirled and danced, droplets hanging in the air like glistening pearls before lashing out in powerful torrents that doused the flames and swept enemies off their feet. The cool, refreshing scent of rain mingled with the harsher stench of battle, offering a momentary reprieve.

Air magic whipped through the streets, carrying whispers of wind that sliced through the combatants with razor-sharp precision. The gusts howled and whistled, lifting debris and scattering it like confetti in a storm. The sharp, metallic tang of ozone filled the air, and static electricity prickled along his skin.

Nero's lightning crackled and danced overhead, casting eerie, flickering shadows across the battlefield. Bolts of raw energy struck with deadly accuracy, their blinding light followed by the deafening boom of thunder that shook the very ground. The scent of singed air and ionized particles was sharp and tangy, adding to the discord of sensory overload.

Despite the overwhelming odds and the mayhem of magic around them, Caelum and Lanae fought with a synchronized elegance, their earth magic providing a solid foundation amidst the chaos. The ground pulsed with life beneath their feet. With each magical cast and swings of their swords, they chipped away at the enemy forces, driven by a fierce resolve to protect their home and each other.

Caelum swung his sword, the clash of steel ringing in his ears as he deflected the next mindless soldier's strike. His muscles tensed, readying for the next attack, but he hesitated as he locked eyes with his opponent. Shock flooded his veins, freezing his movements. His father's face, contorted with malice and void of recognition, stared back at him from beneath the enemy's helm. The man, once a pillar of strength and kindness, now looked at him with nothing but bitter hatred.

Above them, Nero lit up the sky, sending bolts of lightning that crackled and sizzled through the air. The griffin's fierce cries echoed like thunder, each bolt striking with unerring precision. Caelum's father took the brunt of the assault, his body convulsing as black smoke billowed from his nose and mouth, choking him. His sword slipped from his grasp, clattering to the ground with a hollow clang. When he looked up, his eyes mirrored Caelum's, filled with a flicker of recognition and despair.

Caelum gasped, the sudden realization piercing his heart like a dagger. It was a moment he had longed for, to see a glimmer of his true father behind the facade of the mindless soldier. But doubt gnawed at him—he couldn't trust it. Not here, not now.

"Caelum?" His father's voice, though weak and lilting, tore at his soul. The simple question held a world of pain and longing.

Caelum nodded, his throat tight with emotion.

But the moment of connection was brutally shattered. Movement to his right caught his father's attention, and with a sudden burst of strength, his father shoved him back. Caelum stumbled, colliding with another warrior. They both turned in time to witness a mindless minion drive a sword into his father's side. The sickening sound of metal piercing flesh was drowned out by Caelum's shocked cry.

His father's sacrifice ignited a storm of fury within him. The blade had been meant for Caelum, and his father had taken the fatal blow without hesitation. Anger surged through Caelum, raw and unyielding. The ground beneath the soldier's feet rumbled and cracked as Caelum's earth magic erupted. Rocks and debris shot up in an explosive force, shredding the attacker to pieces in a grisly display of power.

The battlefield seemed to pause for a heartbeat, the air thick with the stench of blood, smoke, and earth. Caelum's chest throbbed. His father's sacrifice pressed down on him. But amidst the chaos and pain, a resolve crystallized within him. He would honor his father's memory by fighting with everything he had, to protect those he loved and to defeat the darkness that threatened to consume them all.

He let a battle cry loose from his lungs—a raw, primal sound that echoed through the chaos of the battlefield. The cry tore through the air, reverberating off the buildings and filling the night with its fierce resonance.

The roar surged from deep within him, carrying a fire from years spent in the background, the frustration and determination igniting a fire in his chest. His voice was a powerful force, mingling with the din of clashing steel and the crackling of elemental magic.

Gone was the younger brother relegated to the shadows—in that moment, he was a warrior in his own right, ready to show the world the true extent of his abilities.

# CHAPTER SEVENTEEN
## *Shattered Unity*

THE BATTLE RAGED AROUND Draven, a chaotic symphony of clashing steel, elemental magic, and agonized cries. Frustration surged as he lost sight of Lanae and Caelum in the fray, the press of bodies and the swirl of smoke obscuring them from his view. He couldn't afford to lose focus now—his enemies were relentless, and Alestain's dark magic loomed like a shadow over the battlefield.

He had to get to Alestain. Their only hope was to cut down the man who controlled the masses.

Draven's sword cut through the air, his dragon fire thrumming just beneath the surface. Each strike was precise and powerful, driven by his determination to protect those he loved. He spun around to deflect an incoming blow, only to find himself face-to-face with Alestain.

The dark sorcerer's eyes gleamed with malevolent satisfaction. "So, you are the last Emberwing," Alestain sneered, his voice a silken threat. "Ready to see your family again?"

Draven's grip tightened on his sword. "My family is here in Solstice City."

Alestain's laugh was cold and hollow. "Ah, yes. That feisty wife of yours. I would have preferred her head on a pike at the front of my army, but I'll have to settle for yours." He raised his hands, and dark tendrils of magic coiled around them, crackling with malevolent energy.

Draven braced himself, his muscles tensing as he prepared to face the full force of Alestain's power. The very air vibrated with raw energy, and the ground beneath their feet trembled in anticipation. Heat eviscerated his insides as his fire begged to be let loose. But without the knowledge of where Lanae or Caelum were, he wouldn't resort to flame. He'd just have to use his sword and his wits until he located his family.

A PANG OF ANXIETY rushed through Lanae as she lost sight of Draven and Caelum, the press of bodies and the chaos of battle tearing them apart. The acrid stench of smoke and the metallic tang of blood filled her nostrils, while the clamor of clashing steel and agonized cries echoed in her ears. She pushed forward, her earth magic surging through the ground beneath her feet, causing the earth to tremble in response.

She spun and swung her blade, the clang of metal on metal shuddering up her arm.

Spric's sharp eyes took her in as he pushed her away, a sneer curling his lips. "Oh look, I finally found the one who got away." His eyes gleamed with malicious intent. "I'm tempted to give you the same type of beating I received for letting you get away." He swung his pristine sword in a deadly arc, the blade glinting ominously in the flickering light.

She met his steel and spun out of his reach, her movements fluid and precise. A guttural cry cracked the night, and Caelum's devastation bloomed in her mind, flipping her panic buttons. She had to find Caelum and Draven—but first, she had to deal with the immediate threat before her.

Lanae's grip on her sword tightened, her knuckles turning white. "You're not a killer, Spric. Get out of my way."

Spric laughed, a harsh, rough sound that grated on her nerves. "Oh, but I am." He raised his sword, and the space surrounding him crackled with dark energy, a tangible manifestation of his malevolence.

"Your sword doesn't have a speck of blood on it," she taunted, her voice steady despite the fear gnawing at her insides. She parried his strike, her blade deflecting his with a ringing clash. She stepped in, aiming to take advantage of his momentary imbalance, but his fist shot out with lightning speed.

Before she could dodge, his fist collided with her nose. A fountain of blood flowed out, the sting of it blurring her vision. She coughed, spurting blood from her mouth as she tried to maneuver away from him, but he spun her around and kicked the back of her knee. Pain exploded through her leg; before she hit the ground, his arm clasped around her neck, and he smashed her wrist with the pommel of his sword.

Her weapon clattered to the ground, the sound lost amidst the chaos. Lanae scratched at his arm, her nails digging into his flesh as panic surged through her. The world narrowed to the suffocating pressure on her throat and the desperate need to breathe.

A woman she would have recognized anywhere stepped in front of them, her mother's eyes sharper than they were the last time Lanae saw her. She held her blade out as if to run her through, her expression a mix of determination and sorrow. Lanae's brain fogged from the lack of oxygen, her vision tunneling. She sent a silent prayer to the gods that Draven wouldn't raze the universe when he found her.

CAELUM'S EMOTIONS NUMBED. IF he thought about his father's sacrifice too long, he would falter. Lanae's panic seared through him, and he spun, scanning the crowd for her. In the chaos, he glimpsed Jenna instead and that protective need flared.

She fought like a seasoned warrior, and his heart clenched at the sight of her. They all were fighting for their lives and he couldn't afford to be distracted. He swung his sword, deflecting an attack, but pain exploded in his side as he was struck from behind.

Caelum staggered, his vision blurring as he fell to the ground. He tried to push himself up, but the pain was overwhelming. Jenna's voice reached him through the haze of agony.

"Caelum!" she cried, her voice filled with desperation as she fought to get to his side. She rushed to him, her hands trembling as she tried to stanch the bleeding. "Don't leave me," she whispered, her voice breaking. "Please don't leave me. I love you."

Caelum's heart ached at her words. He reached up to touch her face, his fingers brushing against her tear-streaked cheek. "I love you too, and I don't plan on leaving any time soon," he said through the brutal agony accosting him.

Between being hit and Lanae's fading energy, his frantic need to get to his family surfaced, forcing him to his feet despite his wounds.

ALESTAIN'S MAGIC HIT DRAVEN in a brutal blow, knocking the wind out of him as it pounded his chest to a pulp. He was amazed he still stood against the dark sorcerer's relentless magic. His muscles strained against the onslaught, but he refused to give in. He had to find Lanae and Caelum—he couldn't lose them.

A wave of wind hit from above, and Draven glanced up.

Nero soared over the battlefield, his keen eyes taking in the chaos below. He swooped down, sending bolts of lightning into the enemy ranks, his fierce cries echoing across the battlefield.

But even the mighty griffin wasn't invincible. Alestain sent a blast of dark magic at Nero, and it struck true. Nero's wings faltered, and he plummeted toward the ground. Draven's protective flare demanded he save Nero before the griffin hit the earth, and he bellowed his anguish to the gods above.

# CHAPTER EIGHTEEN
## *Dragon's Roar*

LANAE STARED INTO THE eyes of the woman who raised her with love, the mother she cherished with all her heart. Her vision blurred behind the mist of unshed tears. One escaped out of the corner of her eye, trailing heat down her cheek and catching the faint glimmer of moonlight. The chill of Spric's relentless grip around her throat sent deep muscle shakes down her body. Her head swooned with the dizziness of not enough oxygen, the world narrowing to a pinpoint of pain and fear.

When her mother lunged forward, the sound of her blade meeting flesh was a sickening squelch that echoed through the chaos. Lanae blinked, her mind numb to the anticipated agony. Spric's hold faltered, and as Lanae glanced down, she noticed her mother's blade had sliced through the fabric of her shirt, the cool steel perilously close but miraculously sparing her flesh.

She spun out of Spric's grip, the rush of air filling her lungs with a burning clarity, as her mother withdrew her blade from the enemy's side. The pungent bite of blood mingled with the damp earth and sweat of battle.

"No one harms my daughter."

The snarling declaration, filled with primal ferocity, took Lanae by surprise. She shook the shock from her head and swiped her blade off the ground, the familiar weight in her hand reassuring as more mindless minions surrounded them. Spric stumbled out of the fray, the sound of his ragged breathing lost in the din of clashing swords and desperate cries.

A roar filled the air, a deafening guttural sound that vibrated through Lanae's chest. Her gaze shot to the sky, heart tumbling at the sight of Nero's limp body falling. Before she could scream her denial, a beast surged from the ground. Shimmering scales of green and gold reflected under the pale moonlight as a dragon raced to snatch Nero out of the sky, its wings creating a tempest of wind and dust.

The sight of the mighty beast rising above the fray brought the battlefield to a standstill, as every warrior, both mind-controlled and free, looked to the skies in awe and terror.

Caelum's awe brushed her consciousness like a whisper, laced with an undercurrent of searing pain. Lanae's heart pounded against her ribs as she bolted through the crowd, her mother a fierce shadow on her heels.

The air buzzed with the clash of metal and the shouts of soldiers. Dust and debris swirled around her as enemy soldiers were flung aside by the force of her earth magic, their cries drowned out by the roar of the battlefield. She pushed harder, every step a desperate leap toward the source of that pain.

When Jenna and Caelum, injured and struggling, came into view amidst the chaos, a surge of magic erupted from her fingertips. A path of thick, twisting vines shot forward, carving out a haven in the tumult. The scent of fresh earth and crushed leaves mixed with the acrid odor of smoke and blood, creating a space large enough for Draven to gently lay Nero down.

Lanae and her mother slid into the sanctuary just as the walls of vines closed in around them, cocooning them in a momentary peace that trembled with the violence outside.

CAELUIM TURNED TOWARD LANAE, his eyes heavy with unshed tears. As his gaze landed on their mother's clear, searching eyes, shock and devastation warred within him like twin storms. Her eyes, usually bright with warmth, were now clouded with fear and a desperate need for answers.

"Have you seen your father?" Her fragile whisper pierced through the surrounding chaos.

All fight left him, and he crumbled to the ground next to Nero's unconscious form. The cold, hard earth pressed against his knees, and the distant sounds of the battlefield became a muted roar in his ears. His breath came in shallow, ragged gasps as he fought to hold back the wave of grief threatening to engulf him.

"He saved me." The words left his lips like ice, as cold as the wound in his side that throbbed with every heartbeat. Lanae rushed to him, her presence a soothing balm that warmed the chill gnawing at his bones.

Before their mother could step any closer, Jenna's sword gleamed, its edge a sharp, unforgiving barrier. Jenna's stance was rigid, her eyes blazing with determination as she blocked their mother's advancement. To Jenna, the woman shielded by Lanae's cocoon was the enemy, a threat she was duty-bound to neutralize.

"You'll be okay." Lanae's voice was a fragile whisper as she glanced at Nero. "We'll all be okay." Her denial shone in her eyes, a desperate hope that made him grit his teeth.

"No, Lanae. Dad died saving me."

His voice cut through the air, sharp and jagged, making her recoil as if struck. The raw, unfiltered grief in his tone was a knife twisting in both their hearts.

"If you hadn't noticed, we were losing. There are more Solstice City guards on the ground than the enemy." The reality of their situation overwhelmed him, their losses suffocating.

Lanae shook her head, her wide eyes infused with a blend of fear and defiance. "Draven shifted."

"And what exactly is he going to do? Burn the city down?"

The sharpness in his retort made her eyes widen further, the stark truth of their peril hanging between them like a specter.

DRAVEN SOARED AWAY FROM the safe zone Lanae created, the wind whipping against his scales and the roar of battle echoing in his ears. With Caelum, Nero, and Lanae shielded from the fighting, he could focus on his nemesis. Below, the streets were a chaotic blur of Solstice City soldiers and mind-controlled enemies grappling in desperate combat.

A line of dark magic streaked toward him, its sinister energy crackling in the air. He banked sharply, the force of his maneuver sending a shudder through his wings. Glancing back, he saw the assault battering Lanae's barrier from all sides. A deep, guttural roar erupted from his throat as he unleashed a searing plume of flame, the heat intense enough to turn enemy soldiers to dust.

"No!" Lanae's cry cut through the din, stanching his flame.

He glanced at her, his eyes flashing with frustration as he banked again.

"They are innocent!" Her voice, filled with desperate conviction, rang out.

*This again.* He rolled his eyes, annoyance flaring. Pain suddenly exploded in his side as a direct hit of dark magic sent him veering uncontrollably into the line of buildings. The impact rattled his bones, and he let out a pained growl, the world spinning around him.

Draven shook off the pain as best as he could, his eyes narrowing in on Alestain. With a powerful beat of his wings, he soared toward his nemesis, talons extended. The rush of wind roared in his ears, mixing with the distant cries of battle and the crackling of fires below.

His claws closed around Alestain with a vise-like grip, lifting him off the ground with a surge of triumph. The enemy struggled in his grasp, but Draven held him firm, wings straining as he sped toward the training fields where he could unleash his fire without restraint.

The landscape blurred beneath them, a patchwork of smoke and shadows. As they neared the open expanse of the training fields, a sharp, burning pain sliced through his talon. He glanced down to see Alestain wielding a wickedly curved blade, blood already dripping from the wound he'd inflicted and Alestain's bloody hand pasted to the side of the open laceration.

The dark magic woven into the cut pulsed with a malevolent energy. Draven's vision wavered as Alestain chanted, the words of a blood spell resonating with a sinister power. The magic wrapped around his free will, binding it and making every swish of his wings a struggle.

Fury surged within him, a fire that roared louder than the pain. But the spell was already taking hold, the dark magic coiling around him like a serpent.

He would not be Alestain's might in this war. He'd sooner die than attack Solstice City. As Alestain's dark magic clawed at his very soul, Draven's resolve hardened. With a roar that echoed across the battlefield, he shook Alestain from his grip; the force sent his nemesis plummeting toward the ground. The air whipped around him as he soared higher, every beat of his wings a defiant cry against the curse trying to bind him.

But as Alestain fell, the insidious tendrils of the blood curse tightened their hold, wrapping around Draven like chains of fire. A searing, desperate need to save the falling figure burned through him, an unnatural compulsion that made his heart race with panic. He fought the order with every fiber of his being, but the curse's power was overwhelming.

His body betrayed him, turning against his will. His wings folded in, and with a sickening lurch, he spiraled toward the earth. The wind howled in his ears; the ground rushed up to meet him. The sensation of falling, of losing control, was a terrifying blur of motion and pain.

As he hurtled downward, following the same path as his new twisted master, blood and ash filled his mouth. The dark magic coiled tighter, binding him to Alestain's fate with a merciless grip.

"OH GODS!" LANAE CRIED as Draven flew away. The reflection of Alestain's blade slicing into Draven's talon left her heart blasting a path of ice through her veins, every heartbeat sending a shivering chill. Even from this distance, she recognized the choking scent of the black smoke of a blood curse, its oily tendrils curling into the air.

She turned to her unconscious griffin and then looked at her brother, the urgency in her voice like thunder. "Wake him up—otherwise, we are all dead." She plucked a feather, its soft down fluttering against her fingertips, and then, with a surge of raw magic, blasted the walls surrounding them apart, the stone crumbling and dust swirling in the air.

Fear clawed at her heart, a gnawing beast, as she raced toward the training fields. Draven plummeted headfirst for the ground, the wind howling in his ears, racing to catch his new master. Lanae sent everyone in her path flying back; their startled cries filled the air as she carved her way to her husband. The ground exploded in a flurry of rock and vines, the earth shaking and rumbling, pushing both allies and enemy beyond reach of her.

Draven's claws clamped around Alestain and then tossed him out of the way before he collided with the ground. The impact sent a shudder through the earth, as if it were cracking in two. The sound echoed like a thunderclap. The mighty beast hit with enough force for it to be a killing blow, and Lanae's chest exploded with panic, her breath lodging in her throat and her vision blurring with tears.

She skidded to a stop next to his bleeding talon, the slick mud splattering up her legs. Without conscious thought, she sliced a cut in her palm with the feather quill, the sharp sting followed by blood pooling in her hand. She shoved the feather itself in the cut on Draven's talon, cringing as his hot, sticky blood mingled with hers. Despite a thousand reservations swarming

in her mind, she slammed her bloody palm over
the cut; the wetness seeped between her fingers,
and she uttered the spell Xoltan had whispered
in her ear years ago—the one that made her body
his to manipulate. His voice, still haunting and
cold, echoed in her mind.

Magic lit up Draven's body, an incandescent
glow that spread like wildfire across his scales.
Sparks traveled over his body, crackling and
hissing, and the scrape of bones realigning
whispered in the air, a chilling symphony of clicks
and clacks. A rumbling groan echoed across the
field, a deep, guttural sound that vibrated
through the ground.

"Get up, beast." Alestain's voice echoed from
near Draven's head, authoritative and cold,
cutting through the chaos.

Lanae stiffened, the breath catching in her
throat. When she pulled her hand away from
Draven's scales, the cut that had been there was
fully healed, the flesh knit together seamlessly.
She stared at her palm, blinking in disbelief. A
neat little row of golden scales slashed across her
palm where she had sliced it open, shimmering
with an otherworldly glow.

DRAVEN'S EYES OPENED AS another annoying
kick hit his skull, the jolt sending a sharp pain
through his head. Alestain was ordering him to
get up, his voice grating and relentless. But the
compulsion to do as he demanded was not fully
there. In its place was a warm glow, like Lanae
had wrapped him in her magic, a comforting
embrace that soothed his aching body. Her

lavender scent draped around him, delicate and sweet, as if she stood right next to him, the fragrance enveloping him in a cocoon of reassurance.

He lifted his head, grumbling as he scrambled to get to his feet, the ground beneath him rough and uneven. His body hurt from the impact of the fall; every muscle protested, but not nearly as much as it should have. He had known that kind of fall was deadly, the kind that could shatter bones and crush organs, but somehow, he was alive and not just a broken heap of flesh. The breeze brushing past him was filled with the sounds of the battlefield, the clash of steel and the cries of warriors, a cacophony of chaos that seemed distant and muted compared to the warmth of Lanae's magic.

Movement near his feet pulled his attention, and his heart stalled at the sight of Lanae staring up at him in awe, her eyes wide and shimmering. *She could not be here. Not with Alestain controlling his body.* The memories of Xoltan controlling Lanae flashed in his mind, sharp and painful. Lanae had no defense against a dragon like he had against her blades.

"Kill her!" Alestain's order rang out, a harsh, grating sound, followed by a blast of his dark magic toward Lanae. The air crackled with the malevolent energy, the shadows deepening.

Draven's body coiled with his protective instinct, muscles tensing; a wall of ivy erupted in front of her, the leaves rustling and the vines creaking as they protected her from the blast of Alestain's dark magic.

*Did you do that?*

Lanae's voice filled his head, and he blinked, the warmth of her presence washing over him. *Lanae?*

Her laughter rang out, both in his mind and on the field...a bright, joyous sound. The wall of ivy surrounding her burst into ashes, the embers dancing in the air. Lanae stood with her sword in her hand and a triumphant smile on her gorgeous lips, her confidence radiating.

*I guess I own all of you now.* She opened her palm. The bright line of golden scales down her palm made him tremble, the sight mesmerizing.

"You stupid dragon. I order you to kill my brother's murderer!" Alestain pointed at Lanae, his voice filled with rage and desperation.

Draven turned to Alestain, his eyes narrowing and falling to the clear Dragon's Heart crystal embedded in Alestain's chest plate. Righteous anger filled every cell, and he met Alestain's pompous glare. "I killed Xoltan." His dragon voice rumbled over the field, a low, powerful growl.

Alestain's eyes widened as the ramifications of the order he had just issued crossed over his features. The loss of his mighty weapon before him rang clear in every nuance of his grimace.

"Before you execute that order, kill her and then raze this city to the ground," he bellowed, his voice cracking. The order rippled over the armies, and the mind-controlled soldiers turned from their battles and ran toward the training field with murder in their eyes.

Lanae swept her arm at the edge of the field, and a flaming wall of ivy raised, the heat radiating and the flames crackling, blocking the armies from the training grounds. She glanced up at

Draven with that incredible smile, her eyes sparkling.

*You have my permission to enact the vengeance you've carried for the last century. Do with Alestain as you see fit.*

Her words released him from waiting for orders. And Draven turned his fiery glare on Alestain. Fire built in his chest, the heat intensifying, and Alestain grinned, thinking he was going to end Lanae.

"Did you know a new blood spell could nullify all others?" Lanae called out, her voice strong and clear as she raised her palm, showing him the shiny new dragon scales that reflected iridescent under the moon's rays.

Alestain's gaze snapped to hers, his eyes widening at the meaning.

Fear, as pungent as the piss spreading over the front of his pants, hit Draven's senses just before he blasted Alestain with the full force of his dragon fire, the flames roaring and consuming both the fae and the Dragon's Heart.

A pang of guilt slashed through him at the loss of the relic his family had safeguarded, but without the power of the dragons fueling the thing, it was just a sentimental jewel. When he closed his mouth, nothing was left but scalded ground where Alestain stood. The harsh stench of burned earth filled his nostrils.

Draven turned toward his beautiful wife, his heart swelling with relief and love. "Did you know?"

Lanae raised a shoulder, her expression a mix of pride and nonchalance. "I took a chance." She crossed to stand in front of him, her footsteps light on the scorched ground, and he lowered his snout. Her embrace was warm, her touch gentle, and the wash of kisses over his nose pulled a content grumble from him, the softness of her lips like a balm to his weary soul.

"I'm not sure I like not having free will," he grumbled, his voice a deep rumble. "But you've always commanded me since we first met, so I guess nothing really has changed, except I seem to be able to wield your power and you seem to be able to cast my flames."

"Huh?" She leaned back and stared at him, her eyes wide with surprise.

"You put up that flaming wall of ivy." He nodded to the barrier still in place, the flames flickering and casting a warm glow.

She stared at it, her gaze thoughtful, and then a light, musical giggle escaped her lips. The sound of it was enough to warm his soul. Joy radiated through him. She rubbed his snout, her touch tender and reassuring. "You know, I've always wanted to ride a dragon."

"Your wish is my command." He chuckled, a deep, resonant sound, and lowered himself to the ground so she could climb onto him, the earth cool against his scales. "But you've ridden me many times already."

"Shush." A playful note filled her voice at his innuendo before she climbed onto his shoulders, her hands steady as she settled into place.

The heat of her legs wrapping around his neck sent a thrill through him, a quiver of exhilaration that rippled down his spine. He had never in all his existence seen a fae riding a dragon while they soared through the sky. Her strong and steady heartbeat against his scales made for a powerful vision in his mind, and he hoped it gave Lanae the same sense of invincibility.

As soon as she was settled in place, he stood to full height, his powerful muscles coiling and bunching beneath his scales, and launched into the air. The wind rushed past them, a fierce, exhilarating gale that whipped around them. Her laugh filled him with glee, a joyful melody that echoed in his heart and resonated through his very being.

But the minute they turned toward the city, all their joy fizzled. The sight of flames licking at the sky and smoke billowing was a wake-up call to the battle still ahead. The noxious smell of smoke filled his nostrils, and the sounds of distant cries reached his ears, a somber symphony of war.

THE JOY OF FLYING on Draven's back sent a thrilling jolt through her. The wind whipped her hair out of her face and the softness of his scales beneath her hands spread a delicious heat to her core. But dread clawed at her heart, wiping out all sensations of warmth as she caught sight of Alestain's frozen army, their unmoving forms like a nightmare tableau. The periodic clash of swords drew her attention to the few who fought without Alestain's mind control, the metallic ring hacking through the air. Her gaze zeroed in on Spric, his movements determined and fierce as he fought to get to the field.

Darkness threatened to take her into a downward spiral. Grief clenched her chest. Losing her father echoed in her soul, a deep, abiding ache that refused to be soothed. The knowledge that Spric would soon experience the same crushing blow filled her with profound sorrow, her heart aching for him. The taste of salt lingered in her throat from unshed tears, and the scent of smoke and blood filled her nostrils, the grim realities of war all too present.

Lanae used her earth magic to push soldiers away from Spric, the ground shifting and trembling beneath her command. The soldiers stumbled and cried out; the earth rippled like waves under their feet, creating a space for Draven to land without harming anyone. The scent of freshly turned soil filled the air, mixed with the acrid tang of smoke.

"Please land there," she called out, her voice steady and clear, pointing to the spot she wanted Draven to land. The surrounding air seemed to hum with energy, the magic coursing through her veins.

Draven banked in a slow circle, his wings slicing through the air with powerful strokes. The wind rustled through his scales, and the cadence of his wings beating was a deep, rhythmic thrum. He descended gracefully and landed in front of Spric with a heavy thud, the impact sending a rumbling tremor through the earth.

Spric drew back, his eyes narrowing with rage. When his gaze landed on her, his fury blasted clear in his eyes, the intensity of his anger like a physical force. "You." He aimed his sword at her, the blade gleaming menacingly in the sunlight.

Draven growled, a deep, rumbling sound that vibrated, shifting the surrounding rubble. Smoke billowed from his nostrils, the acrid scent filling the air.

"Yield!" Lanae commanded, her voice strong and unwavering, and pointed her sword at Spric. The gleam of her blade reflected the moonlight, a sharp contrast to the darkness threatening to engulf them.

Caelum stepped into view, his steps steady despite the burden he carried. One arm was draped over Jenna's shoulder, the other over their mother's. Behind him limped Nero, his movements slow and pained. Covering the three of them was a warrior Lanae recognized from the day Spric took her captive, his stance protective and alert.

*Granger,* Caelum's voice announced in her head, the name resonating. They formed a solid line in the event Spric made a run for it. The tension in the air was thick, a silent promise of the battle that could erupt at any moment.

"Let me down," Lanae whispered to Draven.

His discontented growl rumbled through his chest...a low, resonant sound that belied his actions. He lowered himself, the ground trembling under his weight, and she climbed off, the cool night air brushing against her skin. She gave him a kiss on his jowls, her lips warm against the rough texture of his scales, before she stepped in front of him. Draven stood, his massive form casting a shadow in the moonlight, a dark silhouette that paused the rest of the fighting, the eerie quiet punctuated only by the distant sounds of battle.

"Do you yield?" she asked Spric again as she faced him, her voice steady and commanding. The moonlight glinted off her sword, casting a silver sheen over the blade, and her gaze locked onto Spric's.

"Where is my father?" His voice quivered, laden with fear and uncertainty. His eyes darted around, searching for a glimpse of the man who had once loomed so large in his life.

"Answering for his sins in the halls of the gods," Draven said before Lanae could answer, his voice a deep, resonant growl that reverberated through the air.

The words hung heavily, echoing in the silence that followed. The tension was palpable, a sharp, cutting presence, and Draven's statement settled like a heavy shroud over everyone present.

Spric's expression crumbled, the hardness in his eyes melting away to reveal a vulnerable, anguished soul. His glare sharpened through a veil of tears, the salty droplets clinging to his lashes, reflecting the moonlight.

"Yield and release the people from their mind-controlled haze, and we will let you live." Lanae's voice held firm but carried an undertone of compassion. She waved at the figures frozen throughout the city, their lifeless stares a persistent token of the power the Firetwills held over them.

Silence stretched between them, a heavy, suffocating silence that seemed to amplify the distant sounds of the battle, the occasional clash of steel and the muffled cries of the wounded. The night air was cool, carrying the scent of burning wood and the earthy aroma of freshly turned soil.

Draven's imposing form loomed behind Lanae, a silent sentinel, his scales catching the glint of the moonlight. The dragon's eyes, fierce and unyielding, were locked onto Spric, a notice of the unstoppable force that awaited should he refuse.

# CHAPTER NINETEEN
## *A Morbid Conundrum*

SPRIC'S SHOULDERS SAGGED, HIS resolve crumbling like a fragile facade. The situation bore down on him, visible in the tremble of his hands and the way his gaze wavered, unable to meet Lanae's steady stare. The heavy atmosphere crackled with tension as thick as the smoke hanging in the air, suffocating and oppressive. Spric's chest heaved with heavy breaths, each exhale a mix of defeat and bitter acceptance, the sound like a slow, mournful sigh.

Finally, with a shuddering breath, Spric's sword clattered to the ground, the metal ringing out in the stillness—a sharp, lonely sound that echoed in the night. His knees buckled, and he fell to the ground, his head bowed in submission.

The sight of him broken and defeated stirred a complex mix of emotions in Lanae, all of which swirled inside Draven's mind like a tornado.

"I yield," Spric whispered, the words almost carried away by the night breeze.

Lanae nodded, her expression softening as she stepped forward, her sword lowering. "Release them," she commanded, her voice steady yet gentle.

Spric's face tilted up to hers with an expression filled with agony, his eyes wet with unshed tears. "I can't."

The raw honesty in his voice struck Draven, reminding him of Varkir's words after they had beaten Xoltan. *The entire Firetwill line must die to release the masses from their hold.*

Lanae must have remembered the same thing because she glanced back, meeting the dragon's gaze. Her eyes filled with regret, reflecting the injustice of what she might have to do now that Spric surrendered.

Draven's chest squeezed in response to her inner turmoil and the decision bearing down on her.

"Explain," Draven snapped, his voice a deep, commanding rumble that reverberated through the night air.

"I am a shapeshifter like my mother. I did not inherit any of my father's magic." His voice trembled as he glanced around at his father's army, suspended in frozen animation.

Lanae pressed her lips together, her sorrow suffocating, blanketing Draven with a deep sense of melancholy. "Do you have any siblings?" she asked.

He shook his head. "No," he replied, the single word filled with resignation.

Draven grumbled, the sound a low, guttural growl, and traded a glance with Caelum as he shifted back into human form. The transformation was swift, his powerful dragon form morphing into a tall, imposing figure. He reached around and took Lanae's sword from her and stepped forward, sparing her from making this heart-wrenching decision.

"Stand down."

Her sharp command gripped his muscles, freezing them in place. The intensity of her voice was like a physical force, holding him immobile.

He turned his head slowly, his movements stiff, and leveled a knowing stare at her, his eyes dark and piercing. *You know as well as I do what must be done,* he conveyed silently, his gaze unwavering.

She shook her head. "I won't condemn him for his father's actions." Her voice was steady, but the undercurrent of sorrow was unmistakable. The moonlight cast a pale glow over her features, highlighting the firm set of her jaw and the fire in her eyes.

"The council's war tribunal will determine his fate." Lanae's voice was steady and resolute, each word sharp and clear.

"And what of all these people trapped by Firetwill's dark magic?" Draven waved to the masses, his powerful arm carving a path through the air. The spectacle of the countless frozen figures, their eyes vacant and their bodies motionless, stirred a deep sense of urgency within him. The biting odor of lingering dark magic tainted the air.

"He was going to kill you," Lanae's mother said from behind Spric, her voice filled with anger.

A surge of protective instinct flared within Draven at the thought of Lanae being in danger.

Spric tensed, his muscles coiling with latent energy, and his hand moved closer to his sword, the blade glinting in the pale light as if his instincts were screaming at him to fight instead of yield.

*One life for the many.* Draven shot the thought to her, his mind racing. The notion echoed in his thoughts, a pragmatic solution to the dire situation.

"No." Lanae's voice was firm and her stance unyielding. She stood tall, her resolve like a beacon in the darkness.

Although Draven adored her for her principles and compassion, the mental lockdown she had placed on him kept him from taking matters into his own hands. The curse acted like invisible chains, his every instinct demanding action, yet he remained bound by her command. The moment bore down on him, the cool night air doing little to soothe the simmering frustration within.

CAELUM BLINKED AT THE sound of Draven's voice in Lanae's head, the mental link between his sister and the dragon carrying a strange sensation that reverberated through his own mind. The man's frustration blared through the link, a heated surge that made Caelum grit his teeth. He agreed with the dragon. If this asshat's death would awaken the masses, he'd put the bastard down himself.

He shook off Jenna and his mother, their worried hands falling away, and slid his sword out of its scabbard with a sharp, metallic hiss. The mass of the steel in his hand was familiar and comforting. "If you won't kill him, I will," he declared, his voice resolute and edged with anger.

"No, Caelum." Fire sputtered on Lanae's fingertips, tiny flames licking at the air as she put her hand out in a stop signal.

The fire on her fingers wasn't what stalled his breathing. It was the line of scales down her palm that made his eyes just about bug out of his head.

Lanae closed her hand, dousing the unusual flames as she traded a look with Draven.

*Told you.* Draven's voice filtered into her mind, and through the bond Caelum had with her. The sensation was peculiar, a whisper that seemed to brush against the edges of his thoughts.

"What in the..." Caelum started, his confusion evident.

Spric moved, and Draven shot out a plume of fire, the heat intense and scorching, melting the weapon he was reaching for. Burning metal and smoke filled the air.

"Draven," Lanae scolded, her voice sharp.

"I still have some will of my own," he grumbled, glaring at her. "Protecting you overrides the blood curse."

Caelum stared at them, his eyes moving from Lanae to Draven and back. "What blood curse?"

Instead of answering, Lanae's gaze dropped to the weeping wound on Caelum's side. Her brow knit together with concern, and her eyes darted to Nero. The pain from the wound throbbed dully, a reminder of his vulnerability.

"Why haven't you healed him?" she barked at the griffin, her voice sharp and urgent.

Nero squawked at her, the sound a mix of frustration and concern, and he stepped to Caelum's side. The griffin's feathers brushed against the wound, but Caelum did not experience the tingling relief he was used to with the griffin's healing power. Only a minor itch gripped the deepest part of his wound, then nothing.

Nero's gaze landed on Draven in a pointed gesture before returning to Lanae's.

She blinked, her eyes widening with realization. "I used it all on Draven?" she murmured, the words heavy with disbelief.

Nero nodded his head slowly, the seriousness of the situation reflected in his solemn gaze.

"The feather you took?" Caelum asked, then shook his head. "We can worry about that later. What we are going to do with this bastard, that's another story." He pointed his sword at the trembling man, the blade gleaming in the moonlight.

"Caelum," Lanae warned, her voice tense.

"He's the one responsible for beating you. Isn't he?" Caelum's anger flared, the thought of his sister's suffering fueling his rage.

Draven's murderous growl echoed in the air, stilling the remaining fighters. All eyes focused in their direction.

The fact the man at their feet wasn't ashes dug under Caelum's skin. He stared at his brother-in-law, his grip on the sword tightening. "She was black and blue and bloody when she got back. You didn't see the condition he left her in. I did." His voice was thick with emotion, the memory of Lanae's injuries cutting deep.

Draven's gaze shot to Lanae in a pleading way that sunk into Caelum, the silent communication between them a testament to their bond. And the conversation solidified into a horrible thought.

*You're controlling him?* He lobbed the accusation right into her head, the mental link allowing his anger and disbelief to resonate.

She winced and met his gaze in a fleeting look before she glanced at the ground. Shame colored her cheeks, a flush of pink against her pale skin. After witnessing a blood curse and seeing his parents in a catatonic state for years and then having them attempt to kill him with their own hands, Caelum could not abide by his sister's wishes.

"This is war, Lanae. And there will always be casualties." He swung his blade. It whistled through the air, but before it could connect, a lightning bolt hit the sword, shattering it.

Nero let out an ear-splitting cry, the sound piercing the night. Blinding light ripped from him, rolling over the entire city with blasts of lightning. Thunder rumbled overhead—a deep, resonant roar. Bodies dropped to the ground in awe and fear, their eyes wide with terror. The mind-controlled screamed as they held their heads, black smoke billowing from them. Dark magic fled from the white light of the righteous griffin's power.

LANAE GASPED WITH A sharp intake of breath, and she shielded her eyes from the blinding light. When the blast of brightness dissipated, her gaze fell on Nero. He swayed on his feet, his powerful legs trembling, and then his eyes rolled up into his head and he keeled over on his side. The thud of his body hitting the ground reverberated through the air.

"Nero!" Her scream shattered the night, a piercing cry of desperation and fear, and she raced to the griffin's side, her heart rapid-firing in her chest. Draven and Caelum followed close behind, their footsteps heavy and urgent.

With the bulk of everyone's attention on Nero, Spric sprinted toward freedom, his movements quick and desperate. The sight of him fleeing sent a jolt of panic through her, but she was too concerned with Nero to catch him.

Granger stepped into her line of sight and pulled his bow from his shoulder, nocking an arrow with swift precision.

Before she could intervene, Granger let the arrow fly, the twang of the bowstring and the whistle of the arrow slashing through the breeze. A split second before she could get a wall up to protect Spric, the arrow hit true, slicing through the enemy's heart. Even with the wails of the mind-controlled echoing around them, she heard the sickening sound of the arrow piercing Spric's skin, a dull thud that resonated in the silence.

Spric fell to the ground, his body crumpling lifelessly, as her fiery hedges surrounded him, the flames flickering and casting eerie shadows. The scent of burning foliage filled her nostrils, mingling with the metallic tang of blood.

# CHAPTER TWENTY
## *Binding Flames*

THE MOMENT SPRIC DIED, the cries over the city faded as the black magic coating their skin died with him. Draven cast a weary glance around the city, his eyes taking in the sight of people awakening from their suspended animation, their faces etched with confusion and relief. Burned magic permeated the air, lingering over the battle-ridden streets.

Draven reached down and placed his hand on Nero's chest, but only the cool, lifeless feathers radiated under his palm. There was no flutter of a heartbeat, no rise and fall of the beast's chest. The silence was deafening. He pressed his lips together, a tight line of grief, and stepped away, turning his back on Lanae and Caelum as they pleaded with the griffin to wake up. Their desperate voices cut through the night, but he couldn't bear to listen.

His bones tingled with the knowledge of their friend's death, a cold sensation that settled deep within him. The realization that it had been unnecessary, as unnecessary as wasting the griffin's precious healing powers on him, gnawed at him. He glanced toward the field, the memory of his fall vivid in his mind, and a strange noise escaped him, a mix of sorrow and frustration.

The speed of his descent, along with the height he had been falling from, was catastrophic. He should not be standing, much less breathing. That he was alive felt like an anomaly, and his faithful companion had paid the price. The weight of that knowledge was heavy on his heart.

Lanae's hand landed on his arm, her touch warm and grounding. There were too many ifs forming on his lips, too many questions and regrets, and he forced them all down with a swallow. He met her tear-filled gaze, the sadness in her eyes mirroring his own.

"I was dead in that field." The statement crackled with as much fire as the surrounding infernos...a raw, burning truth.

She looked at the field and then back at him. "Your wound was still bleeding." She ran her thumb along his arm in the spot where Alestain's blade had pierced his talon, the touch sending a shock through him. Her chin trembled, and she shrugged. "The bond still tingled when I touched you."

He looked away, unable to bear the confusion and pain in her gaze. "You should have let me end him."

She swung him back around to face her, her grip firm. "Nero did not want the stain of murder on any of our souls." Her whisper caressed him, a gentle balm to his aching heart. "This was not like Alestain or Xoltan. If we had executed Spric, it would have destroyed something good in us."

He closed his eyes, knowing she was right, but losing Nero hurt like a blade to the belly—a deep, twisting pain. "How's your brother?"

She glanced beyond him. "I think he'll be okay. Jenna's doting on him, and she has some experience with healing salves."

Lanae's mother stepped in front of him, her presence commanding. Her imposing figure seemed to cast a shadow over him, and the air grew cooler. The faint scent of lavender lingered in the space between them. Lanae got most of her looks from her mother, but there was a steel resolve in his wife that didn't seem to be in the woman before him.

"You're the dragon that the seer told us of?" her mother asked, her voice filled with awe and curiosity, her eyes piercing through him like daggers.

He gave a curt nod, not trusting his voice while his throat was plugged with emotion, making it difficult to speak. His heart battered his chest, the sound echoing in his ears like the drums of war.

"Mom, this is Draven, my husband." Lanae's voice carried a warm lilt meant to drive away the chill of the surrounding night.

Her mother's eyebrows shot up in surprise. "Your father just said you were fate bound to a dragon," she stammered, and her lips pulled back in a sneer. "Not that you would end up together.

I knew we should have agreed to the deal with Xoltan Firetwill."

Lanae's features hardened and Draven's teeth bared at the sentiment. When he opened his mouth, Lanae hissed, "Don't."

His mouth shut in an audible snap and a low growl formed in his throat. He slashed a glare at Lanae.

Her eyes blazed with intensity, a fierce protectiveness that enveloped Draven. "How dare you even insinuate that Xoltan Firetwill would have made a better choice. Draven is my husband. And you, along with this entire city, can go straight to the underworld if you can't accept it."

The way her mother stumbled over words made his lips tilt up at the corners despite the sorrow laced through his form. "I'm not only her husband, but I am also the king of the dragons." He stared her down, tempted to make her bow to him.

CAELUM GOT TO HIS feet with Jenna's help and wiped the sorrow from his cheeks. The salt of his tears lingered on his skin, a bitter reminder of the grief that still churned in his chest. He crossed to where they stood, each step heavy with fury, and he glared at his mother, his vision tinged red.

"You really shouldn't have dropped that name here." He turned his fiery gaze to his sister. "And you should have let us take care of that thing," he growled, his voice rough like gravel as he pointed to Spric's body sprawled out on the ground with an arrow sticking out of his back.

"Your sister was right," Draven said, his tone calm and measured, a marked divergence to the storm raging inside Caelum. "That would have weighed on you and blackened a piece of your soul."

"Are you making him say that?" he shot at Lanae. His words sliced through the air like a blade.

"Caelum—" Lanae started, but Draven put up his hand, slicing her with a look that shut her up. The tension crackled in the air, palpable and suffocating.

"I still have a mind and a mouth of my own, despite the blood curse. So no, she didn't make me say that. As a matter of fact, I said the same damn thing to her a few minutes ago. But she pointed out that our surly griffin protected us in the only way he knew how. So, for us to not honor that sacrifice is blasphemy." Draven's words were like a hammer, each one pounding against Caelum's resolve, forcing him to confront the painful truth.

Caelum's chin quivered, and he clenched his jaw to stop the emotions from slamming into him like a tossed grenade. Grief threatened to consume him, each breath heavy and labored as he struggled to keep it at bay. He turned to his mother, who watched the interaction with a skeptical expression he remembered from his youth; her eyes narrowed, a flicker of disbelief in their depths.

"I'm sorry about Dad." The words tasted bitter on his tongue.

Draven shot a glance at Lanae, and his whispered question filled Caelum's head, the echo of it reverberating in his mind.

"He recognized me." Caelum's voice cracked, the sound raw and broken. The air thickened, each word catching in his throat. "And then pushed me out of the way of a killing blow." The memory of his father's sacrifice seared into his thoughts, a haunting image that lingered like a ghost, its presence chilling his spine.

He worked his throat through a sandy swallow and turned to Jenna. "This is Jenna, the girl I'm going to marry someday." His eyes met hers, seeing the flicker of surprise and hope dance in her gaze.

Jenna's hand fluttered over her mouth, her breath hitching. The subtle floral scent she carried wafted toward him, grounding him in the present.

"Jenna, this is my mother." Even though his voice carried disdain at the woman who slighted Draven, the introduction seemed to warm the chill that surrounded his mother, melting the icy demeanor as she smiled, greeting the fae with much more warmth and charm than she had Draven. The transformation in her demeanor was as more of a slight to Lanae than acceptance of the girl who made his heart ache.

Lanae took Draven's hand, leading him away as the rest of the Solstice City guards took control of the situation. Caelum hoped that whatever his sister had done to save her dragon wouldn't drive a wedge between her and Draven because he was rather fond of his brother-in-law.

Healing fae swarmed the grounds, offering their potions and patches to the wounded, Caelum included. And as his side knit with the help of magic, Jenna held his hand, unwilling to let go until long after the sun rose and most of the dead had been cleared away.

WHEN THE LAST OF the wounded were tended to and the only task left was removing the dead from the streets, Lanae turned to Draven. "Take me to the last place you truly felt at peace." Lanae's voice drifted over the silence between them, like a gentle caress in the cool night air.

His family home, before the disaster, was where he last found tranquility. The memory brought a pang of loss that tightened his chest. Draven turned to her, his gaze heavy with the past. "It no longer exists." He glanced around at the city that had been built on his family's ashes, the scent of smoke and charred wood still lingering in his mind. He muttered an incantation; the ancient words rolled out of his mouth in a whisper, and a portal opened. He pulled her through, the air crackling with residual magic.

They stepped into their bathroom, the warmth and familiarity of the space replacing the turmoil outside.

"But I can take you to the last place I truly experienced every ounce of your love." He pulled her to his lips and sampled her sweetness, the softness of her mouth against his filling him with a profound sense of belonging. "I am at your command until the day we die, and then I will

249

serve you in the afterlife through eternity," he murmured, his voice a vow as he held her close.

Lanae pulled away, her eyes searching his. "As enticing as it sounds to have you at my beck and call, I like the side of you that challenges me and argues with me, and growls at me in aggravation. And even the one who goes against my wishes. I free you of this blood curse to obey."

A ripple of pure magic zipped through him, his skin tingling. He shook as the warm sensation left him, the bond's release like a weight lifting from his soul.

"Now strip," she commanded in a sultry tone that pumped all the blood to his nether regions.

"You first, my queen." He grinned even as the compulsion to tear his clothes off gripped him. But it had nothing to do with her command, and everything to do with wanting her skin against his.

Unfortunately, the universe wasn't ready for them to be free of strife just yet. A pounding at the front door reverberated through the entire house, each thud sending an irritated itch down Draven's spine. He dropped his head to Lanae's, their foreheads touching, and closed his eyes with a sigh. Her scent, a delicate blend of lavender and earth, mingled with the damp air around them.

"Maybe if we're quiet, they'll go away," Lanae whispered, her breath warm against his ear.

A sudden splintering sound echoed through the house, like a gunshot in the stillness, followed by the heavy thud of multiple footsteps in the hall. Draven's muscles tensed, and a growl ripped from his throat, raw and primal. The bathroom door creaked open, the harsh light from the hallway spilling in, and he locked eyes with the elite guard standing there, his glare cold and unyielding.

"You broke my front door?" Lanae snapped, crossing her arms with haughty defiance.

"You two are requested to appear in front of the council. Now." The guard's tone left no room for argument.

Draven ran his hand over his face. The rough stubble scraped against his palm as his mind balked at the order. The cool air of the bathroom contrasted with the warmth of Lanae's presence beside him. He just wanted to soak in a bath with his wife with no interruptions, letting the soothing water envelop them both.

"I just want a bath," Lanae whined, her voice carrying a note of desperation. "Can you at least give us that?"

Draven's lips tilted in a smirk. It was as if she were in his mind, sharing his exact thoughts.

But the guard was not moved by her plea at all. "Now." The guard's voice was cold and unyielding as he stepped inside the room, his heavy boots thudding against the tiled floor. He reached for Lanae's arm, his fingers nearly reaching her skin.

"If you lay a hand on my wife, I will turn you to dust." Draven's voice was low and menacing, each word dripping with a promise of retribution.

The guard's stern expression morphed into fear, his eyes widening as he pulled his hand back to rest on the pommel of his sword. His entire demeanor changed as he sensed the dangerous path he was walking, Draven's threat hanging heavily in the air.

"There will be time for a bath later," he said in a more conciliatory tone. "But the council said this was an urgent matter that could not wait."

"Fine." Lanae's frustration pulled her lips down into a scowl. She threaded her fingers through Draven's, the touch grounding him as they followed the guards out of the house. "Since you broke our door, can one of you stay to make sure we aren't robbed?" Lanae waved at the splintered front door, her glare sharp and unyielding as she cast it at the guards surrounding them.

They got a nod in return, the guard's helmet glinting in the morning light as one of them peeled off and stood at their doorstep, his posture rigid, guarding the house as Lanae requested. With the city in a state of chaos from the attack, it was a necessary precaution. Smoke clung to the air, blending with the distant cries of the wounded.

They marched in formation, with two in front of them and three behind. Their footsteps echoed off the cobblestone streets. The rhythm of the march seemed more oppressive than liberating. It reminded him of being led to a death sentence as opposed to an inquisition.

Especially after the last time he had appeared before the council, their chambers filled with the icy tension of judgment. Their prejudice of him as a dragon was as tangible as the smoke still settling on the streets. The scent of charred wood and ash clung to his clothes in a bitter testament to the recent destruction. Destruction he had a hand in rendering.

His view of the cityscape from street level was far different than it had been from the skies. From above, the city had looked like a sprawling network of lights and shadows, but down here, the harsh reality of destruction was impossible to ignore. A bank of buildings crumbling sent a shock wave through him, the ground beneath his feet trembling with the force of the collapse.

Those were the same ones that Alestain's magic had slammed him into, and the memory of impact flashed through his mind—the searing pain, the explosion of debris, and the sour tang of smoke filling his nostrils. His jaw dropped at the extent of damage his dragon form had caused, the jagged remains of once-proud structures now lying in ruins.

The Citadel stood unharmed in the center of the city, its imposing structure a stark contrast to the surrounding destruction. As they entered the building, the cool air within washed over them, and a symphony of voices rose in the distance, echoing off the high, vaulted ceilings. The higher they climbed, the more noise greeted them, a blend of anxious whispers and authoritative commands.

Draven's heart hammered against his ribs, each beat a relentless drum in his chest. Lanae's hand tightened around his, her grip grounding him as they stepped into the ornate council chambers. The room was filled to the brim with fae and other beings, their eyes glittering with curiosity and judgment.

Granger, the guard who had killed Spric and whom both he and Caelum had saved, stood in the center of the council room, his armor covered in battle gore. Silence settled around them like a heavy shroud, making Draven's ears ring from the abrupt absence of noise.

Granger cleared his throat, the sound resonating in the quiet space. "I haven't been back in Solstice City for more than a couple of weeks. I had been sent on a secret mission, one requested by Thalorian Nightshade, many years ago."

Draven's gaze landed on Lanae's, and he lifted his eyebrow in a silent question. She shrugged and looked back at Granger.

A rumble of whispering voices filled the room, and even Lanae's mother looked stunned.

"He sent me to find the last dragon. The one being capable of saving his daughter from the grips of pure evil." He glanced over his shoulder at Draven and Lanae. "Unfortunately, I couldn't find the dragon, but he certainly found Thalorian's daughter without my intervention."

"Thalorian never told me this," Lanae's mother snapped.

Granger stared her down. "Considering you were the one who begged him to make the original deal with Firetwill, he didn't think you'd condone my orders."

Her lips thinned as her dagger-like gaze moved to Draven's.

"If it pleases the court, I would like to introduce King Draven Emberwing." He waved at Draven and then dropped to his knee in a formal bow that Draven hadn't seen since his childhood. The rustle of clothing filled the room as all the people at the floor level and in the stands surrounding the council followed Granger's lead.

Draven glanced at Lanae in stunned silence for a beat before he spoke, his voice steady despite the whirlwind of emotions. "And I would like to introduce my queen. Lanae Nightshade Emberwing." He nodded at her and brought her hand to his lips. Although he was still unsure what to think of the display, especially considering none of the council members took a knee, their gazes unwavering and filled with an air of superiority.

"Step forward," Faide demanded, his voice sharp and commanding, cutting through the tension-filled air.

Granger gave them a warm smile that should have calmed his racing heart, but it was not shared with the council running this city. Their gazes were sharp and condescending as they stared down their noses at him.

Draven and Lanae complied, their footsteps echoing against the polished marble floor as they moved toward the middle of the room. The cool, smooth surface beneath their feet contrasted with the heat of the countless eyes fixed upon them. The scrutiny of each council member's gaze scratched like a physical pressure against their skin, assessing and judging.

As they walked, the murmur of whispers from the onlookers filled the room, a low hum of curiosity and speculation. The ornate decorations of the council chamber, with its rich stories carved into the very walls, pressed in around them, giving them an acute sense of solemnity and foreboding. Draven's heart clanged in his chest, each beat resonating in his ears, while Lanae's grip on his hand tightened, her presence both a comfort and a reminder of their shared fate.

Movement to the side caught his attention as Lanae's mother took an empty council seat. Her gaze was unwavering and solemn, her eyes cold and distant, as if the council's judgment did not coincide with the crowd surrounding them. The shuffle of cloth filled the room as people rose, their robes rustling like whispers in the tense silence.

Granger moved behind Draven and Lanae, his presence a steady reassurance. Then the guard did the same, the clink of armor echoing in the quiet chamber. Draven caught sight of Caelum and Jenna joining the ranks behind them, their faces set with determination. The silent show made him wonder whether his time was up and this was an execution and not a coronation. A cold sweat broke out on the back of his neck.

Until he saw Varkir and Jairamon join the pack behind him, their familiar faces bringing a surge of hope. Then a few of the bartenders he regularly saw at Mystic Spirits stepped forward, their expressions resolute. And the girls from Lanae's women's group gave him an encouraging nod.

A shock wave ran through his body, the realization dawning on him. This was a show of solidarity. He blinked back at the scowling council, a newfound strength rising within him.

"Since the skirmish seems to be over, it is time to address your forbidden union." Faide's voice rose over the room, each word dripping with disdain and echoing off the high walls of the council chamber.

Draven unthreaded his hand from Lanae's and crossed his arms, the movement deliberate and defiant. "Your rules on what is allowed and not allowed are archaic." His voice resonated with strength.

"Nevertheless, they are our rules," Faide replied, his tone cold and unyielding.

"And yet you let the Undercity thrive?" Draven threw out the only other thing about the council rule that had burned in him, his eyes blazing with fury. "When dragons oversaw Solstice City, there was a fleeting black market presence. And now it's a haven for the perverse. Where are your rules in that scenario?" His words cut through the air, each syllable sharp and accusatory.

A few of the council members had the sense to look ashamed, their eyes dropping to the floor, their faces flushed with guilt.

"Yet you choose to enforce silly rules on the heart versus those that actually do harm," he continued, his voice rising with passion.

The crowd mumbled with approval, their voices a low rumble of agreement. The scent of sweat and anticipation filled the air, the room charged with the electricity of the moment.

"I do not condone this union with my daughter," Lanae's mother said, her voice cold and unyielding.

"You have no say in this union," Lanae retorted, her tone matching her mother's feral intensity. "You don't get to almost sell me off to a beast like Firetwill and then have a say at who truly holds my heart."

Draven's heart rocked at Lanae's words, a surge of protective anger rising within him. His dragon form simmered just beneath the surface, his muscles tensing as he fought to keep his composure.

Her mother recoiled, the shock evident in her eyes.

"You do not get to force my brother into that mind-control machine and then force me into chains in the bastard's bedroom and get to tell me who I can and cannot love," Lanae continued, her voice trembling with righteous fury.

Draven's jaw tightened, his gaze fixed on Lanae's mother. The memories of Lanae's suffering and the injustices she had endured flooded his mind, fueling his resolve. The council's glaring eyes bore into him, but all he cared about was standing by Lanae's side, supporting her in this moment of defiance.

A few of the council members shifted in their seats, the rustle of fabric and creak of wood filling the tense silence.

"We cannot condone this union," Faide repeated, his voice rising to the rafters, echoing off the high ceilings and reverberating through the chamber.

Caelum stepped forward with narrowed eyes, his gaze piercing. "Why not?"

"Because it is against our laws," Faide replied, his tone cold and authoritative.

"Fae laws, you mean," Draven snapped, his voice piercing through the air with razor-sharp precision. He looked around the building at the different species present in the room. Dwarves with their sturdy forms, their beards bristling with indignation. Elves with their ethereal light casting a soft glow around them. Gnomes with their small statures, their eyes glinting with curiosity. Goblins with their grotesque features contrasting with the elegance of the chamber. Trolls with deep-creased faces looked on with their ever-present scowls, while kobolds' magical potions clinked on their belts. Centaurs stood tall with their proud equine stature, and djinn displayed their intricate markings. Dream-traders, shifters, and even the ogres towering over all of them stood in the ranks. Their varied features and expressions were a testament to the city's diversity. The flickering light from the chandeliers cast shadows across their faces, highlighting the tension crackling in the room.

"Tell me, Faide and dear council members, since when did the fae dictate rules for all the species present in this room?" Draven's challenge was obvious. The murmur of the crowd grew louder as Draven's question resonated with those who had experienced the fae's authority. "Especially since no one other than fae has a seat on the very council that makes these arbitrary laws."

The murmuring of the crowd rose in a low rumble of discontent.

Faide's face turned bright red, his eyes blazing with fury. "I will not tolerate—" he began, his voice trembling with anger.

"Silence!" Draven's growling command shattered the room, the force of it sending racking quakes down everyone's spine. His eyes glowed with righteous flames, the heat of his anger intense. "I once told you I thought this council was doing okay by this city, and I had no intention of stepping in and declaring this a monarchy.”

Hushed whispers filled the room, the tension dense enough to cut with a knife.

“However, my view of the council has changed drastically. Where were you when the masses had to defend this city from Firetwill’s army?”

“We were here monitoring the battle,” Faide said, his voice lacking conviction.

“Monitoring from the safety of your sacred halls?” Draven raised an eyebrow, his gaze piercing. “A good leader heads the charge. A good leader does not hide in wait for the results.”

“And you think you are such a leader?” Lanae’s mother snapped, her voice dripping with contempt.

“Oh hell no,” Draven replied, his tone unwavering and his eyes blazing with conviction. “But your daughter fits that description. She fought for this city even when the council had turned on her. Me, I fought for Lanae, and I always will. I should not lead because I would raze the universe for her and for her alone.”

He scanned the room, his gaze intense, before it landed on Lanae’s mother. The emotions swirling within him were a turbulent storm— anger, love, and fierce determination. “I’ve bled for your daughter, and I would do it again in a heartbeat. I would lie down my life for her,” he declared, his voice cracking with the sentiment. “But I will not relinquish my claim on her because of this council’s asinine rules or your personal prejudices.” His words reverberated through the chamber.

LANAE STARED AT DRAVEN as awe filled her, her eyes wide and shimmering with admiration. Her heart launched into the stratosphere at his adoring words, each one resonating deeply within her soul. The surrounding room seemed to fade into the background. The only thing grounding her was the fierce love she saw in Draven's eyes.

"Lanae once told me her dream was to see this society work together to rule. Where every species has a say in the laws created and enforced in this realm." Draven's words rang through the hall, prompting nods from the gathered crowd. "And if I have to claim this is a monarchy to allow that to happen, so be it," Draven continued, his voice unwavering.

"You do not have the authority—" Faide began, his tone dripping with disdain.

"I beg to differ." Varkir stepped forward and produced an ancient tome from his pocket. He slammed it down on the table next to Draven, the sound echoing like a thunderclap. "Many of you on the council recognize this book, yes?"

A few nodded in answer to his question, their faces pale. Faide was not one of them, his expression dark and unyielding.

"This is the original decree of Solstice City scribed by ancient seers," Varkir declared, his voice filled with reverence. "It states the line of authority in Solstice City. According to the decree, the authority of rule shall be bestowed upon the peacekeepers. They are as follows: the line of the first griffin, the line of the first druid, and lastly, the line of the first dragon."

Hushed whispers erupted around Lanae, the sound like leaves rustling in the wind. Validation swelled her heart with pride as she glanced at Draven.

"If fate has been unkind enough to eliminate these peacekeepers, then Solstice City must be ruled by a council representative of the species living under their protection." Varkir glanced at Draven and then at Lanae before looking back at the council, his gaze as judgmental as theirs.

"I don't see any other species sitting on the council. Do you?" Varkir asked Draven.

Draven smirked, the corners of his mouth lifting in a way that made Lanae's heart flutter. "No. I do not."

"And if I recall correctly, Emberwing is the line of the first dragon, is it not?" Varkir continued.

Draven slowly nodded, his eyes never leaving Lanae's. "Yes, it is."

"So, according to the original decree, this council has been operating against the laws of this realm?" Lanae raised an eyebrow, her voice steady despite the storm of emotions raging within her. Satisfaction surged as the council members squirmed, their authority crumbling in the face of the undeniable truth.

Draven cleared his throat, the sound echoing through the chamber. "It seems I have the ultimate authority, according to the original decree. As such, I dismantle the laws that define barriers around relationships. And I dismantle the council as it stands before us."

The room broke out in a roar of discourse, voices clashing like a storm.

Draven lifted his hand, the motion commanding attention, and silence settled after a minute, the air heavy with anticipation. "I was not finished. By this time next week, I expect to see a representative from each of your groups sitting in this chamber with us."

The council stared at the two of them as if they had sprouted multiple heads, their expressions a mix of shock and disbelief. "Wait just a minute," Faide started, his voice high and indignant.

"For what?" Draven's tone was sharp, the challenge clear.

"Arrest them." Faide waved at Draven and Lanae, his face contorted with rage.

Granger raised an eyebrow, his gaze steady. "I studied history, sir. Even I knew the council was skirting the very laws this city was built on." He pointedly gazed at each member, including Lanae's mother. "If you knew, shame on you. And if you didn't, then your unfamiliarity with our founding rules is worrisome. The only people the guard will be arresting are the ousted members sitting in the revered council seats."

"I think we're just about done here." Draven took Lanae's hand, the ember-like heat of his touch grounding her.

"I still did not give my permission for your marriage," Lanae's mother interjected, her voice tight with disapproval, slicing through the air like an icy blade.

Caelum stepped to Lanae's side, his presence a comforting warmth against her own chilled resolve. "I gave permission for them to marry." His voice rang through the chamber, echoing off the oak walls as his gaze pierced his mother's. The intensity of his words seemed to vibrate in her bones. "And according to the law, as the sole surviving male head of the household, my blessing stands." He glanced at Draven, a hint of a smile playing across his lips. "Besides, I couldn't ask for a better brother-in-law."

They left with the confrontation still thick in the room, but Lanae paused at the door. The scent of old parchment and the woodsy aroma of the Citadel filled her nostrils. "And if you ever wish to be welcomed back into my home, Mother, you'd better fix that attitude."

"It's my home," she stated with her chin jutted out, her eyes narrowing like a predator's.

"Not according to the paid-off deed. It's in our name and has been since the year after you disappeared," Caelum answered, his voice a mixture of finality and disdain. "But you're welcome to visit," he called out over his shoulder, the words hanging in the still air.

Silence fell over the room, thick and oppressive, broken only by the sounds of shuffling feet. As the entourage of support disbanded, Lanae's knotted stomach finally released, the tension draining away like sand through an hourglass.

The moment they stepped out of the Citadel, the cool breeze kissed Lanae's flushed cheeks, and the scent of earth and smoke filled her lungs.

Caelum turned to them, his expression softening. "I'm sorry about how our mother treated you, Draven."

"I'll get over it," he replied, but Lanae sensed his disappointment as acutely as her own, a shared ache in her chest.

"Since we are no longer just soldiers, I guess we should go visit the wounded and start planning what to do with the dead." Lanae scanned the battle-ridden streets surrounding them, the sights of scorched earth and fallen comrades searing into her memory.

Draven grumbled and gave her a burning look that told her exactly where he wanted to be, but he nodded anyway. "What did they do with Nero's body?" he asked Caelum.

"He's with the rest of the dead. They used the cavern you created on the training field for the bodies of our soldiers," Caelum said, his voice heavy with sorrow.

"And what of the enemy soldiers?" Lanae asked. Her heart beat like a rabbit's in her chest.

Both Caelum and Jenna grimaced. "The council ordered their heads put on spikes outside the city gates."

"Absolutely not," Draven growled, his eyes blazing with fury. His gaze moved to Granger. "If there are posts being erected, take them down and bring the bodies to the training field."

Warmth filled her at Draven's words. If he hadn't made the request, she would have. Most of the enemy soldiers were not fighting of their own volition. They should not be treated like true enemies of Solstice City. Spric was another matter, but even he did not deserve to be dismembered and displayed as a warning. "They will have their own burial plot in the fields, separate from our people, but honored nonetheless," Lanae added.

"Yes, Your Majesties." Granger bowed and instructed half a dozen soldiers to follow through on the request, their armor clinking as they moved.

Lanae blinked and watched as the guards marched away. "I don't know if I'll ever get used to being called Your Majesty."

Draven chuckled. "Likewise." He threaded her arm through his and leaned close. "I would have rather gone back to a bath." His eyes glimmered with the promise of what might have been before shuttering down with their current duty.

AS THEY DREW CLOSER to the field, a wave of scents and sights hit Draven with a force he had not prepared for. Instead of funeral pyres, they had a funeral pit full of dead bodies, lined with freshly cut flowers. The stench of death mingled with the cloying aromas of roses, lilacs, and lilies, along with an undertone of spiced oils. Each breath was a mix of sweetness and decay, a haunting signal of both life and death.

Family and friends of the dead gathered, their faces etched with grief and solemnity. The air, thick with mourning and sorrow, pressed its unrelenting burden on Draven's shoulders. As he and Lanae stopped near the head of the trench where Nero lay apart from the rest, the people surrounding them dropped to their knees in respect. Their armor scraping against the earth was like a collective sigh of reverence.

"Please. No kneeling. Not here where we should give the dead our respect rather than me." Draven's voice wavered as he spoke, the raw emotion thickening his throat. He dropped to his knee by Nero's form, his hand trembling as he ran

266

it over the griffin's soft feathers. He plucked a handful of feathers and handed them to Lanae as keepsakes. A familiar and final connection to their loyal companion. "Thank you, my friend. I wish you well in the halls of the afterlife. We will see you again someday."

Draven's heart ached as he stepped back, allowing Lanae and Caelum to say their teary goodbyes. He watched as their faces contorted with grief, their tears mixing with the earth beneath them. The sight tore at his soul, the collective loss enveloping him.

He then moved the griffin into the funeral pit, the weight of Nero's body a physical manifestation of his own emotional burden. As he lowered the griffin into the grave, the mingling scents of flowers and death seemed to fill every part of him, a poignant token of the sacrifices made and the lives lost.

"May you all celebrate victory in the afterlife." Draven's voice rang out over the crowd.

The people responded with a roar, a cacophony of grief and pride that resonated deep within him. A pile of unlit torches sat to the side of a golden bowl of burning oil, their wooden handles rough against the fingers of those who reached for them. One by one, family members grabbed a piece of wood, lit it in the burning oil, and tossed it onto the bodies. The smell of burning wood mixed with the sweet and pungent aromas of flowers and spiced oils, creating a funeral blend that burdened the area.

As soon as the procession ended, Draven stepped close to the burning pit. The heat from the flames warmed his face, contrasting with the chill in his heart. He drowned his lungs with air, filling them with the bitter fumes of smoke and decay. With a powerful exhale, he blew a stream of white-hot flame from one side of the pit to the other, the intensity of the fire rendering the dead to ash almost instantly. The image of flames dancing in the night sky was both a tribute and a farewell, a final act of respect for the fallen.

He turned to Lanae, his eyes meeting hers in a moment of shared sorrow. "Fill it with earth." Emotion flooded his firm voice.

She opened her hands, and the piles of dirt at the edges of the pit responded to her command, rolling onto the ashes in a steady, purposeful motion. The sound of earth covering the remains was a quiet, somber accompaniment to the flames' crackling. The soil, freshly turned and now flat once again, signified not just an end, but a new beginning.

The poignancy of the moment weighed heavily on Draven's heart, signifying the start of a new era. One that he prayed would deliver every single one of Lanae's dreams.

# EPILOGUE
## *The Promise of the Future*

**"I** CAN'T BELIEVE YOU bought out Caelum." Lanae crossed her arms over her chest as she stood in the doorway of her brother's empty room. The air seemed different without Caelum's presence, a mixture of nostalgia and anticipation.

Draven was inside, the scent of freshly polished wood filling his nostrils as he situated a new desk in the space. He looked up at her with a lopsided grin, the light from the window catching the mischief in his eyes. "He said he and Jenna had their own place now, and we would need the space." He gave her a halfhearted shrug, his shoulders relaxing. "And I need a place to work here if you insist on staying in the guard."

Lanae's hand dropped to her protruding belly, the warmth of her growing child spreading a bloom of sweetness in her heart. "Are you sure that's the reason?" Her voice was soft, but the tease was evident.

His laugh echoed off the walls, a rich, comforting sound that filled the empty room. "Okay, maybe I was tired of having to be quiet any time things got heated with us." The room buzzed with their shared laughter, the echoes a promise of the joy and challenges to come.

"I saw my mother today."

The temperature dropped with Lanae's words. His smile faded, the memory of their last encounter still fresh and painful. They hadn't spoken more than a few harsh words since the battle, the tension between them as sharp as a blade. He wondered what vitriol she spewed this time; the thought filled him with dread.

"It seems she's reconsidered and would like to be a part of her grandchild's life." Lanae's voice was soft, almost tentative, the vulnerability in her tone tugging at his heart.

The room closed in around him as he processed her words. The scent of herbs from the garden wafted through the open window. Shadows wavered on the walls, cast by the unsteady light of the fireplace, mirroring the growing unease building in his chest.

Draven's jaw tightened, the muscles in his face working to contain the storm of emotions within. He glanced at Lanae, her eyes reflecting a mix of hope and trepidation. The sight of her, the gentle curve of her belly where their child grew, brought a warmth to his heart even as the news left him conflicted.

"What do you want?" he asked, but he already knew the answer. The hope flickering in her eyes was enough for him to put aside his reservations. Her gaze was soft, filled with a delicate blend of longing and determination that tugged at his heartstrings.

"I would like my mother to be a part of our family," Lanae said, her voice steady yet carrying an undercurrent of vulnerability. The air surrounding them pulsed with the implications of her words. "But I told her I would not tolerate any snideness toward you." She paused, the sincerity in her eyes making his resolve waver. "She agreed. It surprised me, but maybe after observing us on the council and heading up the restoration efforts, she thawed to the reality of us."

Draven's heart softened, the pressure in his chest easing as he looked into Lanae's hopeful eyes. "Then that is what we will do." He crossed the room, the wooden floor creaking softly under his weight, and took her in his arms. The heat of her body against his brought a sense of peace and determination.

"I want you to have every one of your dreams," he murmured, his breath warm against her ear. "And I once told you I'd turn the universe to ash for you. That includes torching my own reservations." Each word represented a promise etched in the space between them.

He sealed his statement with a kiss, his lips meeting hers in a tender, lingering embrace. The taste of her, sweet and familiar, filled him with a renewed sense of purpose that vibrated through him along with their electrical connection. The world outside faded away, leaving the two of them

in a shared moment of tenderness and everlasting
love.

The End

Thank you for reading. If you enjoyed KINGDOM
OF FIRE AND FAE, please consider leaving a
review.

# About J.E. Taylor

Reading books never felt so dangerous!

Explore a world of chilling suspense and fantasy with books that come alive as you read.

J.E. Taylor is a USA Today Bestselling Author, a publisher, an editor, a manuscript formatter, a mother, a wife, a grandmother, a retired business analyst, and a Supernatural fangirl. Not necessarily in that order.

She sat down to write her first book in February of 2007 after her daughter asked:

"Mom, if you could do anything, what would you do?"

From that moment on, she hasn't looked back.

She publishes supernatural suspense, urban fantasy, paranormal romance, and fantasy romance that isn't for the faint of heart.

# You can find J.E. Taylor at the following places:

Website: https://JETaylor75.com

Facebook reader group: https://www.facebook.com/groups/jetcryptkeepers

LinkedIn: https://www.linkedin.com/in/JTaylor8

Bookbub: https://www.bookbub.com/authors/J-E-Taylor

Twitter/X: https://twitter.com/JETaylor75

Instagram: https://www.instagram.com/JETaylor75/

TikTok: https://www.tiktok.com/@JETaylor75